Ambrose Lavendale, Diplomat

by

E. Phillips Oppenheim

Ambrose Lavendale, Diplomat
by E. Phillips Oppenheim

Copyright © 2023

All Rights reserved.
No part of this publication may be reproduced, stored in a retrieval system, or transmitted in any form or by any means, electronic, mechanical, photocopying or Otherwise, without the written permission of the publisher.

The author/editor asserts the moral right to be identified as the author/editor of this work.

ISBN: 978-93-57272-49-0

Published by

DOUBLE 9 BOOKS
2/13-B, Ansari Road
Daryaganj, New Delhi – 110002
info@double9books.com
www.double9books.com
Tel. 011-40042856

This book is under public domain

ABOUT THE AUTHOR

E. Phillips Oppenheim was born on October 22, 1866, in Tohhenham, London, England, to Henrietta Susannah Temperley Budd and Edward John Oppenheim, a leather retailer. After leaving school at age 17, he helped his father in his leather business and used to write in his extra time. His first novel, Expiration (1886), and subsequent thrillers piqued the interest of a wealthy New York businessman who eventually bought out the leather business and made Oppenheim a high-paid director.He is more focused on dedicating most of his time to writing. The novels, volumes of short stories, and plays that followed, numbering more than 150, were about humans with modern heroes, fearless spies, and stylish noblemen. The Long Arm of Mannister (1910), The Moving Finger (1911), and The Great Impersonation (1920) are three of his most famous essays.

CONTENTS

CHAPTER I.
    THE MAN WHO COULD HAVE ENDED THE WAR 7

CHAPTER II.
    THE LOST FORMULA 26

CHAPTER III.
    A DEAL WITH NIKO 43

CHAPTER IV.
    GENERAL MATRAVERS REPAYS 58

CHAPTER V.
    SUSCEPTIBLE MR. KESSNER 71

CHAPTER VI.
    THE MACHINATIONS OF MR. COURLANDER 86

CHAPTER VII.
    THE INDISCREET TRAVELLER 103

CHAPTER VIII.
    THE UNDENIABLE FORCE 121

CHAPTER IX.
    AN INTERRUPTED REVUE 137

CHAPTER X.
    THE SENTENCE OF THE COURT 151

CHAPTER I.
THE MAN WHO COULD HAVE ENDED THE WAR

It was a few minutes after one o'clock—the busiest hour of the day at the most popular bar in London. The usual little throng of Americans, journalists, men of business and loiterers, were occupying their accustomed chairs in one corner of the long, green-carpeted room. Around the bar, would-be customers were crowded three or four deep—many of them stalwart Canadians in khaki, making the most of their three days' leave, and a thin sprinkling of men about town on their way to lunch in the grill-room adjoining. On the outskirts of the group was a somewhat incongruous figure, a rather under-sized, ill-dressed, bespectacled little man, neither young nor old, colourless, with a stoop which was almost a deformity. His fingers were stained to the tip of his nails as though by chemicals or tobacco juice. He held the glass of vermouth which he had just succeeded in obtaining from the bar, half-way suspended to his lips. He was listening to the conversation around him.

'The most blackguardly trick that has ever been known in civilized warfare!' a Canadian officer declared indignantly.

'It's put the lid on all pretence of conducting this war decently,' another assented. 'What about the Hague Convention?'

'The Hague Convention!' a young journalist from the other side repeated sarcastically. 'I should like to know when Germany has ever shown the slightest regard for the Hague Convention or any other agreement which didn't happen to suit her!'

The little man on the outskirts of the group, who had been listening eagerly to the conversation, ventured upon a question. His accent at once betrayed his transatlantic origin.

'Say, is there anything fresh this morning?' he inquired. 'I haven't seen the papers yet.'

The Canadian glanced down at the speaker.

'We were talking,' he said, 'about the use of poisonous gases by the Germans. They started pumping them at us yesterday and pretty nearly cleared us out of Ypres.'

The effect of this statement upon the little man was, in its way, extraordinary. For a moment he stood with his mouth open, the glass shaking between his fingers, a queer, set expression in his pale face. Then his lips parted and he began to laugh. It was a mirth so obviously ill-timed, so absolutely unaccountable, that they all turned and stared at him. There was no doubt whatever that for some reason or other the news which he had just heard had excited this strange little person almost hysterically. His lips grew further apart, the whole of his face was puckered up in little creases. Then, just as suddenly as his extraordinary impulse towards mirth had come, it seemed to pass away. He drained his glass, set it down on the edge of the counter, and, turning around, walked slowly out of the place. The remarks that followed him were not altogether inaudible and they were distinctly uncomplimentary.

'All I could do to keep my toe off the little devil!' the Canadian exclaimed angrily. 'I'd like to take him back with me out into the trenches for a few days!'

A young man who had been talking to an English officer on the outskirts of the group, turned around. He was a tall, well-set-up young man, with a face rather grave for his years and a mouth a little over-firm. He, too, had watched the exit of the stranger half in indignation, half in contempt.

'Who was that extraordinary little man?' he inquired.

No one seemed to know. The waiter paused with a tray full of glasses.

'He's staying in the hotel—arrived yesterday from America, sir,' he announced. 'I don't know his name, but I think he's a little queer in his head.'

The young man set down his glass upon the counter.

'A person,' he remarked, 'who can laugh at such a ghastly thing, must be either very queer in his head indeed, or——'

'Or what, Ambrose?' his companion asked.

'I don't know,' the other replied thoughtfully. 'Well, *au revoir,* you fellows! I'm going in to lunch. Sure you won't come with me, Reggie?'

'Sorry, I have to be back in ten minutes,' the other replied. 'See you to-morrow.'

Ambrose Lavendale strolled out of the room, crossed the smoke-room and descended into the restaurant. At a table in a remote corner, seated by himself, the little man who had been guilty of such a breach of good-feeling was studying the menu with a waiter by his side. Lavendale watched him for a moment curiously. Then he turned to speak to one of the *maîtres d'hôtel,* a short, dark man with a closely-cropped black moustache.

'I shan't want my usual table this morning, Jules,' he announced. 'I am going to sit in that corner.'

He indicated a vacant table close to the little man whom he had been watching. The *maîtres d'hôtel* bowed and ushered him towards it.

'Just as you like, Mr. Lavendale,' he said. 'It isn't often you care about this side of the room, though.'

Lavendale seated himself at the table he had selected, gave a brief order, and, leaning back, glanced around him. The little man had sent for a newspaper and was reading it eagerly, but for a moment Lavendale's interest was attracted elsewhere. At the very next table, also alone, also reading a newspaper, was the most striking-looking young woman he had ever seen in his life. Lavendale was neither susceptible nor imaginative. He considered himself a practical, hard-headed person, notwithstanding the fact that he had embraced what was for his country practically a new profession. Nevertheless, he was conscious of what almost amounted to a new interest in life as he studied, a little too eagerly, perhaps, the girl's features. She was dark, with hair brushed plainly back from a somewhat high and beautifully shaped forehead. Her complexion was pale, her eyes a deep shade of soft brown. Her eyebrows were almost Japanese, fine and silky yet intensely dark. Her mouth, even in repose, seemed full of curves. She appeared to be of medium height and she was undoubtedly graceful, and what made her more interesting still to Lavendale was the fact that, although her manner of doing so was stealthy, she, too, was watching the little man who was now commencing his luncheon.

Lavendale, after a few moments' reflection, adopted the obvious course. He summoned Jules and inquired the young lady's name. The man was able at once to give him the desired information.

'Miss de Freyne, sir,' he whispered discreetly. 'She is a writer, I believe. I am not quite sure,' the man added, 'whether she is not the agent over here of some French dramatists. I have seen her sometimes with theatrical parties.'

Lavendale nodded and settled down rather ineffectively to his lunch. Before he had finished he had arrived at two conclusions. The first was that Miss de Freyne, although obviously not for the same reason, was as much interested in the stranger as he was; and the second that his first impressions concerning her personality were, if anything, too weak. He ransacked his memory for the names of all the theatrical people whom he knew, and made mental notes of them. It was his firm intention to make her acquaintance before the day was over. Once their eyes met, and, notwithstanding a reasonable amount of *savoir faire*, for the moment he was almost embarrassed. He found it impossible to glance away, and she returned a regard which he felt in a way was semi-committal, with a queer sort of nonchalant interest in a sense provocative, although it contained nothing of invitation. At the end of the meal Lavendale had come to a decision. He signed his bill, rose from his place and approached the table at which the little man was seated.

'Sir,' he said, 'I am a stranger to you, but I should like, if I may, to ask you a question.'

Even in that moment's pause, when the little man laid down his newspaper and was staring up at his questioner in manifest surprise, Lavendale felt that his proceeding had attracted the strongest interest from the young woman seated only a few feet away. She had leaned ever so slightly forward. A coffee cup with which she had been toying had been noiselessly returned to its saucer. It was genuine interest, this, not curiosity.

'Say, how's that?' the little man exclaimed. 'Ask me a question? Why, I don't know as there'd be any harm in that. I'm not promising that I'll answer it.'

'I was in the bar a moment ago,' Lavendale continued, 'when they were talking of these poisonous gases which the Germans are using. I heard you ask a question and I heard the answer. You were apparently for the first time informed of this new practice of theirs. Will you tell me why, when you heard of it, you laughed?'

The little man nodded his head slowly as though in response to some thought.

'Sit down, young fellow,' he invited. 'Are you an American?'

'I am,' Lavendale admitted. 'My name is Ambrose Lavendale and I was attached to the Embassy here until last August.'

'That so?' the other replied with some interest. 'Well, mine's Hurn. I don't know a soul in London and you may be useful to me, so if you like I'll answer your question. You thought my laugh abominable, I guess?'

'I did,' Lavendale assented, — 'we all did. I dare say you heard some of the comments that followed you out!'

'It was a selfish laugh, perhaps,' the little man continued thoughtfully, 'but it was not an inhuman one. Now, sir, I will answer your question. I will tell you what that piece of information which I heard at the bar, and which I find in the paper here, means to me and means to the world. Hold tight, young man. I am going to make a statement which, if you are sensible enough to believe it, will take your breath away. If you don't, you'll think I'm a lunatic. Are you ready?'

'Go ahead,' Lavendale invited. 'I guess my nerves are in pretty good order.'

Mr. Hurn laid the flat of his hand upon the table and looked upwards at his companion. He spoke very slowly and very distinctly.

'I can stop the war,' he declared.

Lavendale smiled at him incredulously — the man was mad!

'Really?' he exclaimed. 'Well, you'll be the greatest benefactor the world has ever known, if you can.'

The little man, who had arrived at the final stage of his luncheon, helped himself to another pat of butter.

'You don't believe me, of course,' he said, 'yet it happens that I am speaking the truth. You are thinking, I guess, that I am a pitifully insignificant little unit in this great city, in this raging world. Yet I have spoken the solid truth. I can stop the war, and, if you like, you can help me.'

Lavendale withdrew his eyes from his new acquaintance's face for a moment and glanced towards the girl. Something that was almost a smile of mutual understanding flashed between them. Doubtless she had overheard some part of their conversation. Lavendale raised his voice a little in order that she might hear more. He felt a thrill of pleasure at the thought that they were establishing a mutual confidence.

'I'll help, of course,' he promised. 'In what direction are your efforts to be made?'

The little man paused in the act of drinking a glass of water, squinted at his questioner, and set the tumbler down empty.

'Wondering what sort of a crank you've got hold of, eh?'

Lavendale began to be impressed. The little man did not look in the least like a lunatic.

'Well, it's rather a sweeping proposition, yours,' Lavendale remarked.

'Everything in the world,' the other reminded him didactically, 'was impossible before it was done. Your help needn't be very strenuous. I guess there's some sort of headquarters in London from which this war is run, eh?'

'There's the War Office,' Lavendale explained.

'Know any one there?'

'Yes, I know a good many soldiers who have jobs there just now.'

'Then I guess you can help by saving me time. Do you happen to be acquainted with any one in the Ordnance Department?'

Lavendale reflected for a moment.

'Yes, I know a man there,' he admitted. 'It's just as well to warn you, though, that they're absolutely fed up with trying new shells and powder.'

The little man smiled—a queer, reflective smile, filled with some quality of self-appreciation which seemed at once to lift him above the whole world of crazy inventors.

'Your friend there now,' he asked, 'or will he be taking his British two hours for lunch?'

'He never leaves the building after he gets there in the morning,' Lavendale replied.

Mr. Daniel H. Hurn signed his bill and laid down an insignificant tip.

'You through with your luncheon?' he inquired. 'Right! Then what about taking me along and letting me have a word with your friend?'

'I don't mind,' Lavendale agreed, a little doubtfully, 'but he hasn't very much influence.'

Again the other smiled, and again Lavendale was impressed by that mysterious contortion. He glanced towards the adjoining table. The girl was still watching them closely. Jules, whom she had apparently just summoned, was standing by her side, and Lavendale was convinced that the questions which she was obviously asking, referred to him. He left the room with reluctance and followed his companion through the hall and into a taxi.

'Not sure whether I told you,' the latter remarked, as he seated himself, 'that my name is Hurn—Daniel H. Hurn—and I come from way out west.'

'Glad to meet you, Mr. Hurn,' Lavendale murmured mechanically. 'You are not taking anything with you to show the people at the War Office, then?'

Mr. Hurn shook his head.

'Not necessary,' he answered. 'Bring me face to face with a live man—that's all I need, that's all you need to end the war.'

'I am an American,' Lavendale reminded him.

Mr. Hurn glanced at his companion curiously. Lavendale, dressed by an English tailor and at home in most of the capitals of Europe, was an unfamiliar type.

'Shouldn't have thought it,' he admitted. 'This the place?'

Lavendale nodded and paid for the taxi without any protest from his companion, whom he piloted down many corridors until they reached a room in the rear of the building. A boy scout guarded the door. He stood on one side to let Lavendale pass, but glanced at his companion questioningly.

'Would you mind waiting here just for a moment?' Lavendale suggested. 'My friend is in this room, working with several other men. It would be better for me to have a word with him first.'

'Sure!' the other agreed. 'You run the show. I'll wait.'

Lavendale entered the apartment and approached the desk before which his friend was sitting.

'Hullo, Reggie!' he exclaimed.

The young man, who was hard at work, looked up from a sheaf of papers and held out his left hand.

'How are you, Ambrose? Sit down by the side of me, if you want to talk. We're up to the eyes here.'

Lavendale leaned over the desk.

'Look here, old chap,' he went on, 'I've come on a sort of fool's errand, perhaps. I've got a little American outside. He's a most unholy-looking object, but he wants a word with some one in the Ordnance Department.'

Merrill shook his head reproachfully.

'Is this quite fair?' he protested. 'We've had our morning dose of cranks already.'

'I'm sorry,' Lavendale said, 'but you've got to deal with one more.'

'Know anything about him?'

'Not a thing,' Lavendale admitted. 'I've talked to him for five minutes, and I have just an idea that you ought to hear what he has to say.'

Merrill laid down a paperweight upon his documents.

'Look here, old fellow,' he said, 'I'll take your little pal round to Bembridge, if you say the word, but I warn you, he is as fed up as I am and he'll be pretty short with him.'

'I shouldn't think my man was sensitive,' Lavendale observed. 'Anyhow, my trouble's over if you'll do that.'

Merrill sighed and closed his desk.

'This way, then.'

They passed out of the room to where Mr. Daniel H. Hurn was waiting. Merrill seemed a little taken aback as Lavendale briefly introduced them, and his glance towards his friend was significant.

However, he led them both down the corridor and knocked at a door at the further end.

'Is the General disengaged?' he asked the orderly who opened it.

They were immediately ushered in. Two clerks were seated at a great round table, apparently copying plans. There were models in the room of every form of modern warfare. A tall, thin man in the uniform of a General, was examining some new pattern of hand grenade as they entered.

'Sir,' Merrill began, addressing him apologetically, 'my friend here, Mr. Ambrose Lavendale, who was in the American Embassy for some time, has brought Mr. Daniel Hurn of Chicago to have a word with you.'

The General dropped his eyeglass and sighed.

'An invention?' he asked patiently.

'Something of the sort,' Mr. Hurn admitted briskly. 'Do I understand that you are a General in the British Army?'

'I am, sir,' General Bembridge admitted.

'Very well, then,' Mr. Hurn proceeded, 'I am here to tell you this—I can end your war. When you're through with smiling at me, you'll probably say 'Prove it.' I will prove it. There's a row of taxicabs down below. Take me outside this city of yours to where there's a garden and a field beyond. Afterwards we'll talk business. You'll want to, right enough. It'll take about an hour of your time—and I can end the war!'

There was a moment's silence. The two clerks who had been writing at the table, had turned around. General Bembridge was looking a little curiously at his unusual visitor.

'Mr. Hurn,' he said, 'I will be frank with you. The average number of visitors who present themselves here during the day with devices which will end the war, is twenty. To-day that average has been exceeded. I have already spoken to twenty-four. You make, you see, the twenty-fifth. If we were to go out in taxicabs and watch experiments with every one of them——'

'Pshaw! I'm not one of those cranks,' Mr. Hurn interrupted. 'Read this.'

He handed a half sheet of notepaper across to the General, who adjusted his eyeglass and read. The heading at the top of the notepaper was '*The Chicago School of Chemical Research*' and its contents were brief:

> '*Mr. Daniel H. Hurn is a distinguished member of this society. We recommend the attention of the British War Office to any suggestion he may make.*'

'Here's another,' Mr. Hurn went on. 'This is from the greatest firm of steel producers in the world—kind of personal.'

General Bembridge glanced at the historic name which recommended Mr. Hurn to the consideration of the Government. Then he sighed.

'I am going to-morrow morning at ten o'clock,' he said, 'to inspect a battery at Hatton Park, three miles from Hatfield, on the road to Baldock. You can meet me at the lodge gate at a quarter to ten and I will give you a quarter of an hour.'

'This afternoon would have been better,' Mr. Hurn observed, buttoning up the letters in his coat, 'but to-morrow morning it shall be.'

The General waved them away. Merrill glanced curiously at the American as the three men walked down the corridor.

'Those letters did the trick,' he remarked. 'Forgive me if I hurry, Lavendale. Don't let your friend be a minute late to-morrow morning or he'll lose his chance.'

'I'll see to that,' Mr. Hurn promised. 'Guess I can hire some sort of an automobile to take me out there. Good morning, Captain Merrill,' he added, by way of parting salute, holding out his curiously stained hand. 'I am much obliged to you for your help, and you can sleep to-night feeling you've done more than any man in this great building to save your country.'

Merrill winked at Lavendale as he disappeared within his room. The latter, with the inventor by his side, stepped out into the street.

'About going down there to-morrow morning——' he began.

'Young man,' Mr. Hurn interrupted impressively, 'you've done your best for me and it's only right you should have your reward. You may accompany me to this place, wherever it is.'

Lavendale laughed softly, a laugh which his companion absolutely failed to understand.

'All right,' he agreed, 'I'll take you down in my car. I'll be at the hotel at nine o'clock.'

'At five minutes to ten, if the General is punctual,' Mr. Hurn promised, 'you shall see the most wonderful sight you have ever witnessed in your life.'

II

Punctually at nine o'clock on the following morning, Lavendale brought his car to a standstill before the front door of the Milan Hotel. Mr. Hurn, looking, if possible, shabbier and more insignificant than ever, was waiting under the portico. He clambered at once to the seat by Lavendale's side.

'Haven't you any apparatus to bring, or anything?' the latter inquired.

Mr. Hurn smiled.

'Not a darned thing!'

Lavendale was puzzled.

'You mean you're ready to start with your experiment, just as you are, like this?'

'Sure!' the little man answered, 'and you'd better get her going.'

They started off in silence. Once more Lavendale, as he glanced at the shabby little object by his side, began to lose confidence. As they swung round into Golder's Green he spoke again.

'What sort of a show are you going to give us?' he asked.

Mr. Hurn glanced at his watch.

'You'll know inside of an hour,' he replied.

Lavendale frowned. His protégé's appearance that morning was certainly not prepossessing. His collar showed distinct traces of its vicissitudes upon the previous day. His ugly, discoloured hands were ungloved; his boots were of some dull, indescribable material which seemed to have escaped the attentions of the valet; his flannel shirt was of the style and pattern displayed in Strand establishments which cater for the unæsthetic. He had discarded his hat for a black cloth cap and he had developed a habit of muttering to himself. Lavendale pressed the accelerator of his car and increased its pace.

'I suppose I've made a fool of myself,' he muttered.

They reached the open country and drew up in due time before the lodge gates of what seemed to be a very large estate. There was no sign as yet of the General. Mr. Hurn descended briskly and at once embarked upon a survey of the neighbourhood. Lavendale lit a cigarette and paused to watch the approach of a great limousine car rushing up the hill. It passed them in a cloud of dust,—he stood staring after it. Notwithstanding the closed windows, he had caught a glimpse of a face, of eyes gazing with strained intentness out on to his side of the road—the face of a woman convulsed with urgency—the woman who had played such queer havoc with his thoughts. Almost at the same moment there was a rasping voice in his ear.

'Say, Mr. Lavendale, there's just one thing I ought to have warned you people about, you don't want any spectators to this show. There ain't no one on this earth has seen what you are going to see.'

Lavendale was conscious of a queer flash of premonition. They three—the girl, the crazy little American and he himself—at this critical moment seemed to have come once more together. What was the girl doing out here? Could her appearance really be fortuitous? The little man's warning became automatically associated with this unexpected glimpse of her. Then, with a returning impulse of sanity, Lavendale brushed his suspicions on one side.

'There'll only be farm labourers within sight, anyway,' he remarked. 'You see, no one could have known that we were coming here.'

'That may be so or it mayn't,' Mr. Hurn replied dryly. 'Anyway, I guess this is the boss coming along.'

An open touring car, driven by a man in khaki, drew up at the lodge gate. General Bembridge descended briskly and came towards them, followed by Captain Merrill.

'Glad to see you are punctual, Mr. Hurn,' he said. 'Now, if you please, I am at your disposal for a quarter of an hour. What is it that you have brought to show me?'

'That's all right, General,' Mr. Hurn replied affably. 'You don't need to worry. I've been taking my fixings round here. Just step this way.'

He shambled along across the turf. The others followed him, the General walking by Lavendale's side.

'Hasn't your friend brought any apparatus to show us?' he inquired irritably. 'What's he going to do?'

'Heaven knows, sir!' Lavendale replied. 'He has told me nothing. If it weren't for those letters he showed you, I should have thought he was a lunatic.'

Mr. Hurn assembled the little party about twenty-five yards ahead of a fringe of trees which bordered the road-side and terminated after a slight break in a compact little spinney. He turned to Captain Merrill.

'Say, young man,' he suggested, 'you just hop round the other side and make sure there's no one about.'

Merrill, in obedience to a glance from the General, hurried off. The latter turned towards Mr. Hurn.

'You are leaving us very much in the dark, sir, he remarked. 'What is it that you propose to attempt?'

'I propose to accomplish on a small scale,' Mr. Hurn said grandiloquently, 'a work of destruction which you can repeat upon any scale you choose. See here.'

With the utmost solemnity he drew from his pocket a schoolboy's ordinary catapult and a pill-box. From the latter he selected a pellet a little smaller than a marble. He fitted it carefully into the back of the catapult. Captain Merrill, who had completed his tour of the spinney, returned.

'There is no one about, sir,' he announced.

Mr. Hurn had suddenly the air of a man who attempts great deeds. His attitude, as he stepped forward, was almost theatrical. The General had become very stern and was obviously annoyed. Lavendale's heart was sinking fast. He was already trying to think out some form of apology for his share in what he felt had developed into a ridiculous fiasco. Nevertheless, their eyes were all riveted upon the strange little figure a few feet in front of them. Slowly he drew back the elastic of the catapult and discharged the pellet. It struck a tree inside the spinney and there was immediately a curious report, which sounded more like a slow muttering of human pain than an ordinary detonation. Mr. Hurn pointed towards the spinney. There were great things in his attitude and in his gesture. A queer, very faint, grey smoke seemed to be stealing through the place. There was a sound like the splitting of branches amongst the trees, the shrill death cries of terrified animals. The General would have moved forward, but Mr. Hurn caught him by the belt.

'Stay where you are, all of you,' he ordered. 'The place ain't safe yet.'

The wonder began to grow upon them. The various shades of green in the spinney seemed suddenly, before their eyes, to change into a universal smoke-coloured ashen-grey. Without any cause that they could see, the bark began to fall away from many of the trees, as though unseen hands were engaged in some gruesome task of devastation. The little party stood there, spellbound, watching this mysterious cataclysm. Mr. Hurn glanced at his watch.

'You can follow me now,' he directed. 'With this strong westerly wind you won't need respirators, but breathe as quietly as you can.'

They followed him to the edge of the spinney. There was not one of them who was not absolutely dumbfounded. Every shred of colour had passed from the foliage, the undergrowth and the hedges. Flowers and weeds, every living thing, were the same ashen colour. The ground on which their footsteps fell broke away as though the life had been sapped from it. There were two rabbits, a dead cock pheasant, the glory of his plumage turned into a sickly grey, and a dozen smaller birds, all of the same ashen shade. Lavendale kicked one of them. It crumbled into pieces as though it were the fossil of some creature a thousand years old.

'The pellet which I discharged from the catapult,' Mr. Hurn announced, in his queer, squeaky voice, 'contained two grains of my preparation. Shells can be made to contain a thousand grains. I reckon that this spinney is eighty yards in area. I will guarantee to you that within that eighty yards there is not alive, at the present moment, any bird or insect or animal of any kind or description. Just as they have died, so would have any human being who had been within this area, have passed away. The rest is a matter of the multiplication table.'

'But will your invention bear the shock of being fired from a gun?' the General asked eagerly.

'That is all arranged for,' Mr. Hurn replied. 'I have some trial shells here. The powder, which is my invention, is of two sorts, separated in the shell by a partition. They are absolutely harmless until concussion breaks down that division. This little matter,' he added, waving his hand upon that scene of hideous desolation, 'is like the bite of a flea. A dozen boys with catapults could destroy a division. With two batteries of guns, General, you could destroy ten miles of trenches and a hundred thousand men.'

They walked around the spinney, still a little dazed with the wonder of it. Suddenly Lavendale gave a little cry. Out in the field on the other side lay the motionless body of a woman. They all hurried towards it.

'I thought you came round here, Merrill!' the General exclaimed.

'I did, sir,' the young officer replied. 'There wasn't a soul in sight.'

Lavendale was the first to reach the prostrate figure. Almost before he stooped to gaze into her face, he recognized her. There were little flecks of grey upon her dress and she was ghastly pale. Her eyes, however, were open, and she was struggling helplessly to move.

'I am all right,' she assured them feebly. 'Has any one—any brandy?'

She tried to sit up, but she was obviously on the point of collapse. Mr. Hurn pushed his way to her side. From another pill-box which he had withdrawn from his pocket, he took out a small pellet and forced it unceremoniously through her teeth.

'I invented an antidote whilst I was about it,' he explained. 'Had to keep on taking it myself when I was experimenting. She's only got a touch of it. She'll be all right in five minutes. What I should like to know is,' he concluded suspiciously, 'what the devil she was doing here, any way.'

The recovery of the young lady was almost magical. She first sat up. Then, with the help of Lavendale's hand, she rose easily to her feet. She pointed to the spinney.

'What on earth is this awful thing?' she faltered.

No one spoke for a minute.

'What were you doing round here, young lady?' Mr. Hurn asked bluntly.

She looked at him with her big, innocent eyes as though surprised.

'I was motoring along the road,' she explained, 'when I saw you stop,' she went on, turning towards the General. 'I remembered that I had heard there was to be a review here. I thought I might see something of it.'

There was a silence.

'Perhaps,' Merrill suggested, 'the young lady will give us her name and address?'

She raised her eyebrows slightly.

'But willingly,' she answered. 'I am Miss Suzanne de Freyne, and my address is at the Milan Court. I haven't done anything wrong, have I?'

'Nothing at all,' Lavendale assured her hastily. 'It's we who feel guilty.'

'But what does it all mean?' she demanded, a little pathetically. 'I was just walking across the field when suddenly that happened. I felt as though all the strength were going out of my body. I didn't exactly suffocate, but it was just as though I was swallowing something which stopped in my throat.'

'Capital!' Mr. Hurn exclaimed, his face beaming. 'Most interesting! Perhaps, after all,' he went on complacently, 'if we may take it for granted that the young lady's presence is entirely accidental, her experience is not without some interest to us.'

'But will no one tell me what it means?' she persisted.

There was a silence. Lavendale was suddenly oppressed by a queer foreboding. The General took Miss de Freyne courteously by the arm and led her on one side. He pointed with his riding whip to the gate where the limousine was standing.

'Young lady,' he said, 'Captain Merrill here will take you back to your car. You will confer a great obligation upon every one here, and upon your country, if you allow this little incident to pass from your mind.'

She laughed softly. Her eyes seemed to be seeking for something in Lavendale's face which she failed to find. Then she turned away with a shrug of the shoulders and glanced up at Captain Merrill.

'I am not a prisoner, am I?' she asked. 'Let me assure you all,' she declared, with a little wave of farewell, 'that I never want to think of this hateful spot again.'

They watched her pass through the gate and enter the car which was standing in the road.

'Does any one know her?' the General inquired.

'She was at the next table to Mr. Hurn here when I spoke to him at the Milan,' Lavendale observed thoughtfully. 'She was listening to our conversation. It may be a coincidence, but it seems strange that she should have been on our heels just at this particular moment.'

The General passed his arm through Mr. Hurn's.

'The Intelligence Department shall make a few inquiries,' he promised. 'As for you, my dear sir, our positions are now reversed. My time is yours. I will find another opportunity to inspect these troops. Will you return with me to the War Office at once?'

'Right away,' Mr. Hurn assented. 'And, General,' he went on, swaggering a little as he shambled along by the side of the tall, alert, military figure—queerest contrast in the world—'give me a factory—one of your ordinary factories will do, all your ordinary appliances will do, but give me control of it for one month and you can invite me to Berlin to the peace signing.'

*****

At about half-past eight that evening, after having waited about for some time in the hall of the Milan Grill-room, Lavendale handed his coat and hat to the vestiaire and passed into the crowded restaurant. A young man of excellent poise and balance, he was almost bewildered at his own sensations as he elbowed his way through the throng of waiters and passers-by. At the corner of the glass screen he paused. The girl was there, seated at the same table, with a newspaper propped up in front of her. Her black hair seemed glossier than ever; her face, unshadowed by any hat, a little more pallid and forceful. A fur coat had fallen back from her white shoulders. She seemed to be wholly absorbed in the paper in front of her.

'A table, monsieur?' a soft voice murmured at his elbow.

Lavendale shook off his abstraction and glanced reluctantly away.

'I am dining with Mr. Hurn, Jules,' he replied. 'He said eight o'clock, but I can't see anything of him.'

Jules pointed to a table close at hand, evidently reserved for two people. There were *hors d'oeuvres* waiting and a bottle of wine upon the ice.

'Mr. Hurn ordered dinner for eight o'clock punctually, sir,' he announced. 'I have been expecting him in for some time.'

The girl, as though attracted by their voices, had raised her eyes. She looked towards the unoccupied table by the side of which Jules was standing. The three of them for a moment seemed to have concentrated their regard upon the same spot, and Lavendale was conscious of a queer little emotion, an unanalyzable foreboding.

'The gentleman ordered a very excellent dinner,' Jules observed. 'I have already sent back the cocktails twice.'

Lavendale glanced at the clock. Almost at the same time his eyes met the girl's. There was a quiver of recognition in her face. He took instant advantage of it and moved towards her.

'You are quite recovered, I trust, Miss de Freyne?'

She raised her eyes to his. Again he felt that sense of baffling impenetrability. It was impossible even to know whether she appreciated or resented his question.

'I am quite recovered, thank you,' she said. 'You have seen nothing more of our queer little friend?'

'Nothing at all,' she told him.

'He invited me to dine with him,' Lavendale explained, 'at eight o'clock punctually. I have been waiting outside for nearly half an hour.'

She glanced at the clock and Lavendale, with a little bow, passed on.

'Perhaps he meant me to go up to his room,' he remarked, addressing Jules. 'Do you know his number?'

'Eighty-nine in the Court, sir,' the man replied. 'Shall I send up?'

'I'll go myself,' Lavendale decided.

Jules bowed and, although Lavendale did not glance around, he felt that the girl's eyes as well as the man's followed him to the door. He rang for the lift and ascended to the fourth floor, made his way down the corridor and paused before number eighty-nine. He knocked at the door—there was no reply. Then he tried the handle, which yielded at once to his touch. Inside all was darkness. He turned on the electric light and pushed open the door of the sitting-room just in front.

'Mr. Hurn!' he exclaimed, raising his voice.

There was still no reply,—a strange, brooding silence which seemed to possess subtle qualities of mystery and apprehension. Lavendale had all the courage and unshaken nerves of youth and yet at that moment he was afraid. His groped along the wall for the switch and found it with an impulse of relief. The room was flooded with soft light—Lavendale's hand seemed glued to the little brass knob. He stood there with his back to the wall, his face set, speechless. Mr. Daniel H. Hurn was seated in an easy-chair in what appeared at first to be a natural attitude. His head, however, had fallen back, and from his neck drooped the long end of a silken cord. Lavendale took one step forward and then paused again. The man's face was visible now—white, ghastly, with wide-open, sightless eyes....

The valet, who was passing down the corridor, paused and looked in at the door.

'Is there anything wrong, sir?' he asked.

Lavendale seemed to come back with a rush into the world of real things. He withdrew the key from the door, stepped outside and locked it.

'You had better take that to the manager,' he said. 'I will wait outside here. Tell him to come at once.'

'Anything wrong, sir?' the valet repeated.

Lavendale nodded.

'The man there in the chair is dead!' he whispered.

CHAPTER II.
THE LOST FORMULA

The two young men stood side by side before the window of the Milan smoke-room—Ambrose Lavendale, the American, and his friend Captain Merrill from the War Office. Directly opposite to them was a narrow street running down to the Embankment, at the foot of which they could catch a glimpse of the river. A little to the left was a dark and melancholy building with a number of sightless windows.

'Wonder what sort of people live in that place?' Merrill asked curiously. 'Milan Mansions they call it, don't they?'

The other nodded.

'Gloomy sort of barracks,' he remarked. 'I've never seen even a face at the window.'

'There's a new experience for you, then,' Merrill observed, pointing a little forward,—'a girl's face, too.'

Lavendale was stonily silent, yet when the momentarily raised curtain had fallen he gave a little gasp. It could have been no hallucination. The face, transfigured though it was, in a sense, by its air of furtiveness, was, without a doubt, the face of the girl who had been constantly in his thoughts for the last three weeks. He counted the windows carefully from the ground, noted the exact position of the room and passed his arm through his friend's.

'Come along, Reggie,' he said.

'Where to?'

'Don't ask any questions,' Lavendale begged. 'Just wait.'

They left the hotel by an unfrequented way, Lavendale half a dozen paces ahead. Merrill ventured upon a mild protest.

'Look here, old chap,' he complained, 'you might tell me where we are off to?'

Lavendale slackened his speed for a moment to explain.

'To that room,' he declared. 'Didn't you recognize the girl's face?'

Merrill shook his head.

'I scarcely noticed it.'

'It was the girl whom we found unconscious, half poisoned by that fellow Hurn's diabolical invention,' Lavendale explained. 'She wasn't there by accident, either. I caught her listening in the Milan Grill-room when Hurn was talking to me, and the day after the inquest she disappeared.'

Merrill laid a hand upon his friend's arm.

'Even if this is so, Lavendale,' he expostulated, 'she probably doesn't want us bothering over here. What are you going to say to her? Pretty sort of asses we shall look if we blunder in upon her like this.'

Lavendale continued to climb the stairs. By this time they had reached the second landing.

'If you feel that way about it, Merrill,' he said, 'you can wait for me—or clear out altogether, if you like. I want to have a few words with this young lady, and I am going to have them.'

Merrill sighed.

'I'll see you through it, Ambrose,' he grumbled. 'All the same, I'm not at all sure that we are not making fools of ourselves.'

They mounted yet another flight. A crazy lift went lumbering past them up to the top of the building. Lavendale paused outside a door near the end of the passage.

'This should be the one,' he announced.

He rang a bell. They could hear it pealing inside, but there was no response. Once more he pressed the button. This time it seemed to them both that its shrill summons was ringing through empty spaces. There was no sound of any movement within. The door of the next flat, however, opened. A tall, rather stout man, very untidily dressed, with pale, unwholesome face and a mass of ill-arranged hair, looked out.

'Sir,' he said, 'it is no use ringing that bell. The only purpose you serve is to disturb me at my labours. The flat is empty.'

'Are you quite sure about that?' Lavendale asked.

'Absolutely!'

'How was it, then, that I saw a face at one of the windows a quarter of an hour ago?' Lavendale demanded.

'You are mistaken, sir,' was the grim reply. 'The thing is impossible. The porter who has the letting of the flat is only on duty in the afternoon, and, as a special favour to the proprietors, I have the keys here.'

'Then with your permission I will borrow them,' Lavendale observed. 'I am looking for rooms in this neighbourhood.'

The man bowed and threw open the door.

'Come in, sir,' he invited pompously. 'I will fetch the keys for you. My secretary,' he added, with a little wave of his hand, pointing to a florid, over-buxom and untidy-looking woman who was struggling with an ancient typewriter. 'You find me hard at work trying to finish a play I have been commissioned to write for my friend Tree. You are aware, perhaps, of my—er—identity?'

'I am sorry,' Lavendale replied. 'You see, I am an American, not a Londoner.'

'That,' the other declared, 'accounts for it. My name is Somers-Keyne—Hamilton Somers-Keyne. My work, I trust, is more familiar to you than my personality?'

'Naturally,' Lavendale assented, a little vaguely.

The dramatist, who had been searching upon a mantelpiece which seemed littered with cigarette ends, scraps of letters and an empty tumbler or so, suddenly turned around with the key in his hand.

'It is here,' he pronounced. 'Examine the rooms for yourself, Mr.— —?'

'Lavendale.'

'Mr. Lavendale. They are furnished, I believe, but as regards the rent I know nothing except that the myrmidon who collects it is unpleasantly persistent in his attentions. If you will return the key to me, sir, when you have finished, I shall be obliged.'

'Certainly,' Lavendale promised.

The two young men opened the door and explored a dusty, barely-furnished, gloomy, conventional little suite, consisting of a single bedroom, a boxlike sitting-room, and a bathroom in the last stages of dilapidation. The rooms were undoubtedly empty, nor was there anywhere any sign of recent habitation. Lavendale stood at the window, leaned over and counted. When he drew back his face was more than ever puzzled. He looked once more searchingly around the unprepossessing rooms.

'This was the window, Reggie,' he insisted.

Merrill had lost interest in the affair and did not hesitate to show it.

'Seems to me you must have counted wrongly,' he declared. 'In any case, there's no one here now, and it's quite certain that no one has been in during the last hour or so.'

Lavendale said nothing for a moment. He examined the flat once more carefully, locked it up, and took the key back to Mr. Somers-Keyne's room. The dramatist opened the door himself.

'You were favourably impressed, I trust, with the rooms?' he inquired, holding out his hand for the key.

'I am not sure,' Lavendale replied. 'Tell me, how long is it since any one occupied them?'

'They are dusted and swept once a week,' Mr. Somers-Keyne told him, looking closely at his questioner from underneath his puffy eyelids, 'and they may have been shown occasionally to a prospective tenant. Otherwise, no one has been in them for nearly a month.'

'No one could have been in them this morning, then?'

'Absolutely impossible,' was the confident answer. 'The keys have not been off my shelf.'

'We must not interrupt you further,' Lavendale declared. 'I shall apply for a first night seat when your production is presented, Mr. Somers-Keyne.'

'You are very good, sir,' the other acknowledged. 'Your face, I may say, is familiar to me as a patron of the theatre. What are the chances, may I inquire, of your taking up your residence in this building?'

'I have not made up my mind,' Lavendale replied. 'There are some other particulars I must have. I shall call and interview the hall-porter this afternoon.'

'If a welcome, sir, from your nearest neighbour is any inducement,' Mr. Somers-Keyne pronounced, 'let me offer it to you. My secretary, too, Miss Brown—I think I mentioned Miss Brown's name?—is often nervous with an empty flat next door. I am out a great deal in the evening, Mr. Lavendale. My work demands a constant study of the most modern methods of dramatic production. You follow me, I am sure?'

'Absolutely,' Lavendale assured him. 'By the by, sir, we are returning for a moment or two to the bar at the Milan. If you will accompany us——'

Mr. Somers-Keyne was already reaching out for his hat.

'With the utmost pleasure, my dear young friends,' he consented. 'The Milan bar was at one time a hallowed spot to me. Misfortunes of various sorts—but I will not weary you with a relation of my troubles. If Tree rings up, Flora, say that I shall have finished the second act tonight. You can tell him that it is wonderful. Now, gentlemen!'

They left the building together and a few moments later were ensconced in a corner of the bar with a bottle of whisky and some tumblers before them. Lavendale helped his guest bountifully. He had hard work, however, to keep the trend of the conversation away from the subject of Mr. Somers-Keyne's early triumphs upon the stage, which it appeared were numerous and remarkable. With every tumblerful of whisky and soda, indeed, he seemed to grow more forgetful of his home across the way. As he expanded he grew more untidy. His tie slipped, his collar had flown open, his waistcoat was spotted with the liquid which had fallen from the glass in his unsteady efforts to lift it to his lips. His pasty face had become mottled. Lavendale, who had been watching his guest closely, fired a sudden question at him.

'You don't happen to know a Miss de Freyne, do you?' he inquired innocently.

The change in the man was wonderful. From a state of maudlin amiability he seemed to be stricken with an emotion of either fear or anger. His eyes narrowed. He set his glass down almost steadily, although he was obliged to breathe heavily several times before he spoke.

'Miss de Freyne,' he repeated. 'What about her?'

Lavendale pointed towards the window behind them.

'Nothing except that when I was in here an hour ago I saw Miss de Freyne's face at the window of that empty suite next to yours,' he said.

Mr. Somers-Keyne rose to his feet. A splendid dignity guided his footsteps and kept his voice steady.

'Sir,' he pronounced, 'I am able to surmise now the reason for your excessive hospitality. I wish you good morning!'

He turned towards the door.

'Mr. Somers-Keyne,' Lavendale began, rising hastily to his feet—

The dramatist waved him away. His gesture, if a little theatrical, was final. The honours remained with him....

Lavendale, a few minutes later, on his way to his luncheon-table in the grill-room, threw his accustomed glance across the room towards the corner which was still possessed of a peculiar interest for him. He paused in the act of taking his place. At her same table, with a little pile of manuscript propped up in front of her, Miss de Freyne was seated, studying the luncheon menu. For a moment he hesitated. Then he rose to his feet and, crossing the room, addressed her.

'Miss de Freyne!'

She glanced up in some surprise. She seemed, indeed, scarcely to recognize him.

'You have not forgotten me, I hope?' he continued. 'My name is Lavendale.'

'Of course,' she assented slowly. 'You were the friend of that strange little creature with the marvellous invention, weren't you?'

'I was scarcely his friend,' Lavendale corrected, 'but I did my best to help him.'

She made a pencil mark in the margin of the manuscript and laid it face downwards upon the table. Then she leaned back in her chair and looked at him.

'Tell me what happened?' she begged. 'I was obliged to leave London the next day and I have only just returned. Was it suicide or murder?'

'The man was murdered, without a doubt,' Lavendale replied.

'Is that so, really?' she asked gravely. 'Tell me, had he given over his formula to the War Office?'

Lavendale sighed.

'Unfortunately no! He was to have handed it over at eleven o'clock the next morning.'

'Was it found amongst his effects?'

'Not a written line of any sort.'

'Is any one suspected?' she inquired, dropping her voice a little.

Lavendale hesitated and glanced cautiously around.

'Scarcely that,' he answered, 'but you remember the man Jules, the *maîtres d'hôtel* here?'

She nodded.

'A Swiss, wasn't he? I was just wondering what had become of him.'

'During the investigations the next day,' Lavendale continued, 'it was discovered that his papers were forged and that he was in reality an Austrian. He was interned at once, of course, and I believe there was a certain amount of secrecy about his movements on that night. So far as I know, though, nothing has been discovered.'

She raised her eyebrows deprecatingly.

'The detective system over here,' she remarked, 'is sometimes hopeless, isn't it?'

'Yet in one respect,' Lavendale pointed out, 'they certainly were prompt on that night. I understand that Jules was interned within an hour of the discovery of the murder.'

Miss de Freyne drew her manuscript towards her with a little shrug of the shoulders.

'They failed to find the formula, though,' she reminded him.

Lavendale, accepting his dismissal, returned to his place, finished his lunch and made his way round to the Milan Mansions. A caretaker was established now in his office in the hall. He was a small and rather melancholy-looking man, who hastily concealed a blackened pipe as Lavendale entered.

'I understand that you have a suite to let,' the latter began, 'upon the third floor?'

The man pulled out a list.

'We have several suites to let, sir,' he replied; 'nothing upon the third floor, though.'

'What about number thirty-two?'

The caretaker shook his head.

'Number thirty-two is let, sir.'

'Are you sure?' Lavendale persisted. 'I called this morning and was allowed to look over it by Mr. Somers-Keyne, who had the keys.'

'It was taken by a young lady just before one o'clock, at our head office,' the man told him. 'With regard to the other suites, sir — —'

'Could you tell me the young lady's name?' Lavendale interrupted.

'I haven't heard it yet,' the man answered shortly. 'With regard to the other suites — —'

Lavendale slipped a coin into his hand.

'Thank you,' he said, 'there is no other suite in which I am interested for the moment.'

He stepped out. Almost on the threshold he met Miss de Freyne, face to face.

'Are you coming,' he asked, raising his hat, 'to take possession of your new abode?'

She was entirely at her ease. She looked at him, however, a little curiously. It was as though she were trying to make an appreciative estimate of him in her mind.

'I suppose,' she observed, with a little sigh, 'that we are playing at cross-purposes. You are an American, are you not, Mr. Lavendale?'

'I am,' he answered.

'German-American?'

'No!'

'English-American?'

'No!'

'What then?'

'American.'

'Tell me exactly what that means?' she insisted.

'It means that my sympathies are concentrated upon my own country,' he answered. 'Those prefixes—German-American or English-American—are misnomers. Wherever my personal sympathies may be, my patriotism overshadows them. Now you know the truth about me. I am an American for America.'

She sighed.

'Yes,' she murmured, 'I had an idea that was your point of view. I am a Frenchwoman, you see, for France.'

'Our interests,' he remarked, 'should not be far apart.'

'If I were sure of that,' she declared, 'the rest would be easy. I am for France and for France only. You are for America, and, I am afraid, for America only.'

'Chance, in this instance,' he ventured, 'has at any rate made us allies.'

'I should like to feel quite sure about that,' she said. 'If you are not busy, will you walk with me on to the Embankment?'

They strolled down the narrow street and found a seat in the gardens.

'Between thieves,' she continued, looking him in the face, 'there is sometimes honour. Why not amongst those who are engaged upon affairs which, if not nefarious, are at least secret? Let us see whether we can be allies, and, if not, where our interests clash. You know perfectly well, as I do, that Jules murdered that little chemist from Chicago and stole the formula. You know very well that the suite in which you take so much interest in the Milan Mansions, belongs to Jules. You know very well that he was arrested there a quarter of an hour after he left the hotel, and that he had had no time to dispose of the formula. You know that the place has been searched, inch by inch, but that the formula has not been found.'

'I have just arrived exactly as far as that myself,' Lavendale assented mendaciously.

'You are some time behind me, but it is true that we have arrived at the same point,' she continued. 'Now the question is, can we work together? What should you do with the formula if ever it came into your possession?'

His lips tightened.

'I cannot tell you that,' he said firmly.

'I believe that I know,' she went on. 'Well, let me put you to the test.'

She opened a black silk bag which she was carrying, a little trifle with white velvet lining and turquoise clasp. From a very dainty pocket-book in the interior she drew out a crumpled sheet of paper, covered with strange, cabalistic signs. She smoothed it out upon her knee and handed it to him.

'Well,' she exclaimed, 'there it is! Now you shall tell me what you are going to do with it?'

His hand had closed over the piece of paper. He gripped it firmly. Before she could stop him he had transferred it to his own pocket. She shrugged her shoulders.

'You had better return it to me,' she advised.

'I shall not,' he replied. 'Forgive me. I did not ask you for the formula—I did not know you had discovered it—but since I have it, I want you to remember that it was the discovery of an American and I shall keep it for my country.'

'But your country is not in need of anything of the sort,' she protested.

'I will be so far frank with you as to explain my motive,' he said. 'A few months ago I was attached to the American Embassy here. I have been attached to the Embassy in Paris, and for two months I was in Berlin. I have come to certain conclusions about America, in which I differ entirely from the popular opinion and the popular politics of my country. England has been living for many years in great peril, but there have been many who have recognized that. The peril of America is at least as great, and has remained almost altogether unrecognized. We have no army, a small navy, an immense seaboard, wealth sufficient to excite the cupidity of any nation. And we have no allies. We make the grave and serious mistake of ignoring world politics, of believing ourselves outside them and yet imagining ourselves capable of protecting the interests of American citizens in foreign countries. That is where I know we are wrong. I have resigned from the Diplomatic Service of America but I remain her one secret agent. I intend to keep this formula for her. She will need it.'

Suzanne de Freyne shook her head.

'You will not be able to leave the gardens alive with it,' she assured him.

He glanced at her incredulously. Her smooth face was unwrinkled. She had the air of looking at him as though he were a child.

'You are in the kindergarten stage of your profession,' she observed. 'Now watch. You see those two men seated on the bench a little way further down?'

'Well?'

She rose from her seat, shook out her skirt and sat down again. The two men, also, had risen and were advancing towards them. She held up her hand—they seemed somehow to drift away.

'I repeat,' she went on, 'that you would not leave this garden alive. But, my friend, we will not quarrel over a worthless scrap of paper, for that is precisely what you have carefully buttoned up in your pocket-book. I have failed to find the formula. That is a dummy. Keep it, if you will. There isn't a single intelligible sign upon it.'

He drew it from his pocket and glanced at it. Even with his slight knowledge of chemistry he was compelled to admit that her words were truth.

'Keep it or give it me back, as you like,' she continued. 'It has no value. The fact remains that in his brief journey from the service room at the Milan Grill-room to his rooms in the Milan Mansions, Jules managed to conceal somewhere or other the paper which he has taken from Hurn. If he passed it on to some one else, it is by this time in Germany, but we have reason to know that he did not. The paper is still in concealment. It is still to be found.'

'And the means?' he asked.

She shrugged her shoulders lightly.

'Alas!' she exclaimed, 'how can I tell you now? How can I even engage your help? You have disclosed your hand.'

He sat gazing gloomily out at the river.

'Very well,' he decided at last, 'let me help and I will be content with a copy of the formula.'

She smiled.

'That is rather sensible of you,' she said. 'To tell you the truth, I require your help. For reasons which I need not explain, we do not wish this matter to be dealt with in any way officially. I am in perfect accord with the English Secret Service, but we do not wish to have their men seen about the Milan Mansions. To-night, Jules re-enters into possession of his rooms. I offer you an adventure. It is what you wish?'

'But I thought Jules was interned?'

'He was and is,' she told him, 'but the greater powers are working. This afternoon he will be permitted to escape—he thinks through the agency of friends. He will come to London in a motor-car, he will come at once to his rooms, and, although every inch of them has been searched, I am perfectly convinced that somewhere in them or between them and the Milan, he will lay his hands upon the formula. You care about this adventure?'

His eyes flashed.

'Care about it!' he repeated enthusiastically.

She smiled and rose to her feet.

'Leave me now,' she begged. 'I want to speak to one of those men for a minute. You can dine with me in the Grill-room at the Milan at seven o'clock, in morning clothes. Till then, *au revoir!*'

*****

The spirit of adventure warmed Lavendale's blood that night. He ordered his dinner with unusual care, and he was delighted to find his guest sufficiently human to appreciate the delicacies he had chosen and the vintage of the champagne which he had selected. Their conversation was entirely general, almost formal. They had both lived for some time in Paris and found mutual acquaintances there. As they neared the conclusion of the meal she was summoned to the telephone. She was absent only for a short time but when she returned she began to collect her few trifles.

'The car passed through Slough,' she said, 'a quarter of an hour ago. I think perhaps we had better be moving.'

Lavendale signed his bill and they left the hotel together.

'Nothing else you think you ought to tell me, I suppose?' he remarked, as they crossed the narrow street. 'I am rather in the dark, you know. The idea is, isn't it, that Jules is coming up to get the formula from some hiding-place in his room? Where shall we be?'

'Wait,' she begged.

They climbed the stairs in silence—the girl had purposely avoided the lift. Arrived on the third floor, she passed the door of number thirty-two and knocked softly at the adjoining one. There was, for a moment, no answer. At the second summons, however, the door was cautiously opened. The untidy secretary admitted them. In her soiled black dress, shapeless and crumpled, with her fat, peevish face and dishevelled peroxidized hair, she was by no means an attractive object. She pointed half indignantly to where Mr. Somers-Keyne was lying upon the couch, gazing towards them in incapable silence with a fatuous smile upon his lips.

'If it's from you he gets the money for this sort of thing,' she said sharply, 'why, I wish you'd keep it, and that's straight. How are we to get on with our work or anything, with him in that condition?'

'Scondition'sh all right,' Mr. Somers-Keyne insisted, making a weak effort to rise.

Miss de Freyne frowned for a moment as she appreciated the situation. Then she waved him back.

'Don't try to get up, Mr. Somers-Keyne, she begged. 'We can manage without you. Lie down and rest for a little time.'

Mr. Somers-Keyne sank back with a sigh of content.

'Very shorry,' he murmured. 'Tree'sh awfully annoyed with me. Promised go down and shee him sh'evening.'

'Is this fellow one of your helpers?' Lavendale asked.

She nodded.

'In a small way. Never mind, we don't need him to-night. Come here.'

She led him to the side of the wall nearest the adjoining apartment. Her fingers felt about the pattern of the paper. Presently she found a crack, pushed for a moment and a sliding door rolled back. She stretched out her hand through the darkness and turned a small knob. A wardrobe door swung outwards. They looked into the shadowy obscurity of the adjoining room. Lavendale whistled softly.

'This is all very well,' he said, 'but how can we watch Jules whilst the door is closed?'

She pointed to two or three little ventilation holes near the top of the wardrobe. Lavendale applied his eye to one of them and nodded.

'That's all right,' he admitted. 'There's just enough light. Listen!'

They could both of them hear the quick, eager footsteps of a man lightly shod, stealthy, ascending the last flight of stairs. Her fingers gripped his arm for a moment. An excitement more poignant than any begotten by their hazardous adventure suddenly thrilled him. The greatest adventure of all was at hand....

The footsteps paused, the door slowly opened. It was Jules who entered. He stood looking around for a moment, then unexpectedly fingered the switch which stood upon the wall. The apartment was flooded with light. Jules stood in the centre of it, distinctly visible. He was paler even than usual, and his eyes were a little sunken, but he had lost, somehow or other, that bearing of graceful servility which had distinguished him in his former avocation. An expression of subdued cunning had taken its place. He looked around the apartment searchingly. His eyes rested for a moment upon a small print at the further end of the room, which was hanging upon the wall in a crooked position. As his eyes fell upon it, he frowned. He seemed suddenly to stiffen into a new attention. He glanced once more around him as though in fear and picked up his overcoat from the bed. Before they could realize what his intentions were, he had left the room, closing the door behind him.

'What does that mean?' Lavendale whispered.

She pushed open the wardrobe door. A little breath of fresher air was grateful to both of them. Then she turned and pointed towards the opposite wall.

'It was that print,' she murmured. 'It must have been a signal to him that he was being watched. You see, it is on one side. I am perfectly certain that when I was here this morning it was straight.'

'A signal from whom?'

She had no time to answer him. They could hear the door of the next room open. Their eyes met.

'Mr. Somers-Keyne!' he exclaimed.

They stepped back into the wardrobe. Her fingers felt for the spring. Suddenly they both heard, within a few inches of them, on the other side of the wall, the sound of a click. She pressed the spring in vain. Then she stepped back and turned on the electric light in the room.

'Try the door,' she whispered.

Lavendale tried it. As they both expected, it was locked. She drew a master-key from her pocket and opened it swiftly. They were out in the corridor now, empty and silent. They could not even hear the sound of any one moving about in Mr. Somers-Keyne's room. Lavendale stood before the latter's door and listened. There was a mumbling as though of smothered voices, then suddenly an angry exclamation.

'Sick of the lot of you, that's what I am! Here's the old man dictates his rubbish for about an hour a day and talks drivelling, drunken piffle for the rest of it! Where's my salary coming from, that's what I want to know?'

They heard Jules apparently trying to soothe her.

'My dear Miss Brown, in a few days, if you will only be patient— —'

'Patient! Who's going to be patient with that old drunkard blithering around all the time? I've had enough!'

They heard the sound of stamping footsteps and Mr. Somers-Keyne's sonorous voice.

'Flora, my dear, mosht unreasonable, I'm sure. Shimply asked you go out for a few minutes while Mr. Jules and I dishcuss important matter.'

'And I'm going out for a minute,' Miss Brown shouted, suddenly opening the door, 'and you may thank your stars when you see me again!'

She appeared upon the threshold, holding a slatternly hat upon her head with one hand and sticking hatpins in with the other. She stared insolently at Lavendale and his companion, and brushed her way past them.

'Here's visitors for you,' she called out over her shoulder. 'You'll have to get rid of them now before you start on your precious business.'

She flopped down the stairs. The newcomers stepped across the threshold. Jules stared at them in surprise. Mr. Somers-Keyne nodded his head ponderously. His mind seemed to be still running upon Miss Brown's departure.

'A mosht ungrateful young woman,' he declared. 'Mish—er—de Freyne, your shervant. Thish gentleman is the tenant of the roomsh you looked over other day. Mr. Lavendale, don't like you. Don't want you here. Ashked me questions about you, Mish de Freyne. Not a nice young man at all. You lishen to me a moment.'

He staggered to his feet. Jules stood in the background. There was something of the old obsequiousness about his manner. Mr. Somers-Keyne swayed for a moment upon his feet. Then Lavendale felt a sudden inspiration. He turned on his heel.

'Excuse me for one moment,' he whispered to the girl by his side.

He turned away with no show of haste, though the eyes of both men seemed to follow him. Then he ran down the stairs on tiptoe, taking them three at a time as he neared the ground floor. The motor-car was drawn up outside, there was no sign of any one else in the street. He sprang to the other side of the way and saw at once the object of his pursuit, hurrying down towards the Embankment. He followed her as stealthily as possible. Without looking around she increased her own pace, crossed the Embankment and leaned for a moment over the wall. A few yards further on were the steps and a little pier, and close by a small tug was waiting. Lavendale, who was within reach of her now, stretched out his hand and seized her shoulder.

'I want you, Miss Brown!' he exclaimed.

She turned and confronted him, her face mottled and flushed with the unusual exercise, a strand of her unwholesome-looking hair hanging down to her shoulder.

'Now what's wrong with you?' she shouted. 'Can't you leave me alone? I'm not coming back.'

'Where are you going?' he asked.

'That's none of your business,' she snapped. 'Let me pass.'

He glanced at the tug and his hand closed upon her wrist. He was a strong man, but she almost succeeded in wrenching herself free.

'Look here, Miss Brown,' he said, 'the game's up. I want that paper you're keeping for Jules.'

She suddenly showed her teeth. Her face was like the face of a wild animal. She struggled so violently that they swayed towards the parapet. Her left hand slipped into the bosom of her gown. Before he could stop her, her fingers were making pulp of the paper which she had drawn up in crushed fragments. She threw it over the parapet into the black water. Then she ceased to struggle. She laughed hysterically and leaned back against the wall. The water near where the fragments of paper had fallen was all churned up — the little tug had hurried off.

'Clever, ain't you?' she mocked. 'Any need to hold on to me any more?'

He released her wrist. The car had come thundering down the little street. It suddenly pulled up with a grinding of brakes. Suzanne sprang lightly out.

'The formula?' she cried.

He pointed downwards to the water.

'Destroyed!'

Her sigh was almost one of relief.

'Was there a tug here?' she asked eagerly.

He nodded.

'It made off when they saw us struggling.'

'He told the truth, then!' she exclaimed. 'Jules shot himself as soon as he realized that the game was up — there in the room before me, a few minutes ago. He told me with his last breath that the formula was on its way down the river to Germany.'

Lavendale smiled grimly.

'It's on its way down the river, right enough,' he assented, 'but I don't think it will reach Germany.'

CHAPTER III.
A DEAL WITH NIKO

Lavendale paused in the act of struggling with his tie, and looked steadfastly into the mirror in front of him. He had heard no definite sound, yet some queer intuition seemed to have suddenly awakened within his subconscious mind a sense of the mysterious, something close at hand, unaccountable, minatory. His flat was empty and the catch of the front door secure, yet he knew very well that he was being watched. He turned slowly around.

'What the mischief— —'

He broke off in his sentence. A small man, dressed in black clothes, imperturbable, yellow-skinned, and with Oriental type of features, was standing to attention, a clothes-brush in his hand. His dark, oval eyes rested for a moment upon the crumpled failure of Lavendale's tie. Without a word he took another from an open drawer, came softly across the room and reached upwards. Before Lavendale knew what was happening, the bow which had been worrying him for the last five minutes was faultlessly tied. He glanced into the mirror and was compelled to give vent to a little exclamation of satisfaction.

'That's all very well, you know,' he said, turning once more around. 'The tie's all right, but who the devil are you, and what are you doing in my rooms?'

The man bowed. Again the Oriental seemed to assert itself in the subtle ease with which he almost prostrated himself.

'Sir,' he explained, 'I am the friend of your servant Perkins.'

'Then perhaps you can tell me where on earth Perkins is?' Lavendale demanded.

'He is in the hospital, sir,' the man answered. 'He met with a slight accident while he and I were together. I am his messenger. I undertook to bring you news of him and to do what I could, in my poor way, to fill his place for this evening. He lent me his key. It was in that manner I was able to gain entrance here.'

'An accident?' Lavendale repeated. 'What sort of an accident?'

'I chose an idle word, perhaps,' the other confessed. 'It was indeed more a matter of sudden illness. Perkins and I lunched together at the Chinese Restaurant in Piccadilly Circus. As we left the place, he faltered; he fainted in the passage. I called a taxicab and took him to the hospital. It was not a great affair, they said, but it was better that he should rest there. So I came to you.'

'And who the dickens may you be?'

'My name is Niko. I came from Japan with General Kinish, military attaché to the Japanese Embassy. He has gone to the Italian Front and left me without a situation.'

'You're all right at ties, any way,' Lavendale admitted, glancing once more into the mirror. 'All the same, I think I can get along without a man until Perkins comes back.'

His hands sought his trousers pockets but Niko shook his head gravely.

'It is impossible,' he protested. 'Perkins may be away for a week. I shall wait upon you until he returns. It is best.'

'Well, have it your own way,' Lavendale remarked. 'Better answer that bell, then. If it is a lady, show her into the sitting-room.'

Niko glided away and returned in a moment.

'The lady,' he announced, 'is in the sitting-room.'

He held up Lavendale's coat and the latter hastened from the room. Suzanne de Freyne was standing facing the door as he entered, her theatre cloak thrown back. He took her hands.

'You are adorably punctual!' he exclaimed.

'Tell me,' she asked, a little abruptly, 'how long have you had your valet?'

'About five minutes, I believe,' he answered. 'He is a substitute. My own man was taken ill at luncheon-time. Why do you ask?'

'Because he is the first person,' she explained, 'who has succeeded in puzzling me in one particular way since I can remember.'

He looked at her as though for an explanation, and in a moment she continued.

'I flatter myself that I never forget a face. Your valet is perfectly well-known to me and yet I cannot tell you who he is.'

Lavendale glanced uneasily towards the door.

'I shan't keep him,' he said. 'I hate prejudices, but I am full of them. The fellow's a Jap, of course.'

Suzanne did not reply for a moment. Her attention seemed to have suddenly wandered. Then she turned around with a little laugh.

'I am hungry, my friend!' she exclaimed. 'Let us go. And yet, remember this. Temporary servants are bad things for people who follow our profession.'

They left the room. Niko was standing with the front door wide open, his master's hat and gloves in his hand.

'I will be here at seven o'clock in the morning, sir,' he promised, 'and bring news of Perkins.'

Lavendale nodded. The door was closed softly behind them. At the bottom of the stairs he glanced up.

'Wish I could get rid of the ridiculous idea I have about that fellow,' he remarked.

'Is there anything in your rooms of particular—I will not say value, I will say interest?' she inquired.

'I suppose I have the usual amount of valuables,' he admitted, 'but Perkins is a very careful servant, and I am sure he would never have sent any one who wasn't reliable. As regards my papers and that sort of thing, they are all locked up in a safe with a combination lock.'

She did not pursue the subject and it faded quickly from Lavendale's mind. They dined in a quiet corner at the Milan and they talked of many things, chiefly the war.

'Do you realize,' he asked her, towards the end of their meal, 'that you are still a complete mystery to me?'

She nodded affably.

'Yes?'

'You know what I mean, of course,' he went on. 'Three weeks ago we joined hands for a moment. We were—may I not use the word?—

associates. We were not, perhaps, completely successful in our enterprise, but at least we prevented that marvellous secret from ever reaching an enemy's hands. Then you disappeared. I heard nothing from you until your voice startled me down the telephone to-night—you want to dine with me. Well, I am your slave and here I am, but tell me, where have you been all this time?'

'In France,' she answered.

'And what have you been doing?'

'Attending to my own business.'

'And what is that?' he asked coolly.

She raised her eyebrows but her air of offence was obviously assumed. She lit a cigarette and watched the smoke for a minute. He was absorbed in the study of her hands—her unusually firm yet delicate fingers, ringless save for one large, quaintly-cut emerald.

'In my life,' she said, 'I have no confidants.'

'That seems a pity,' he replied. 'We might be useful to one another.'

'I am not so sure,' she answered thoughtfully. 'For instance, although we speak together in English, my soul is French. I am for France and France only. England is our very dear ally. England is a splendid and an honourable nation, but it is France's future welfare in which I am concerned, and not England's. You, on the other hand, are Saxon. England and America, after all, are very close together.'

'Greatest mistake of your life,' he assured her. 'I have a great respect for England and a great liking for English people, and I believe that she was dragged into this war without wanting it, but, on the other hand, as I told you once before, I am for America and America only. England has asked for what she is getting for a good many years. If even she gets a good hiding it won't do her any harm.'

'But America is so far outside,' she observed.

'Don't you make any mistake,' he answered promptly. 'The world grows smaller, year by year. The America of fifty years ago has become impossible to-day. We have our political interests in every country, and, however slow and unwilling we may be to take up our responsibilities, we've got to come into line with the other great Powers and use the same methods.'

'You may be right,' she confessed. 'Very well, then, you are for America and I am for France. Now tell me, as between Germany and England how are your sympathies?'

'With England, without a doubt,' he pronounced. 'Mind, I am not a rabid anti-German. I am not in the least sure that a nation with the great genius for progress that Germany has shown is not to some extent justified by taking up the sword to hew a larger place in the world for her own people. But that does not affect my answer to your question. My sympathies are with England.'

She flicked the ash from her cigarette. She was looking a little languidly across the room towards a table set against the wall.

'If your sympathy were a little stronger,' she remarked quietly, 'I could show you how to render England an incalculable service.'

'Tell me how?'

'First of all,' she continued, 'look at those three men and tell me what you think of them?'

He turned a little in his place and glanced towards the table which she had indicated. One of the three men who were seated at it was obviously a foreigner. His hair was grey towards the temples, although his moustache was almost jet-black; his cheek-bones were high, his teeth a little prominent. He wore evening clothes of the most correct cut, his shirt and links were unexceptionable. His two companions were men of a different stamp. The one who seemed to dominate the party was a huge man, clean-shaven, with puffy face and small eyes. He wore a dark flannel suit of transatlantic cut. He was drinking a large whisky and soda and smoking a cigar, and had apparently eaten nothing. His companion was of smaller build, with flaxen moustache and hair, and dressed in light grey clothes and yellow boots. On the face of it, the trio were ill-assorted.

'Well, I should say,' Lavendale remarked, 'that the dark man in the corner chair was a foreigner—a Russian, for choice. The other two are, of course, American business men. The face of the big man seems familiar to me.'

'You've probably seen his picture in the illustrated papers,' she told him. 'That is Jacob P. Weald. He was once called, I believe, the powder king.'

Lavendale nodded. His manner had become more interested.

'Of course,' he murmured. 'And that's Jenkins, the secretary to the Weald Company. I wonder who the third man is?'

'His name is Ossendorf—the Baron Cyril Ossendorf. He is a *persona grata* at the Russian Embassy and he owns great estates in Poland.'

'Stop!' Lavendale exclaimed. 'This is getting interesting. He is buying munitions, of course.'

'Marvellous!' she murmured.

'Don't chaff me—it's really interesting.'

'Yes,' she admitted, 'it is interesting even from its external point of view. You are right. The Baron is probably giving, or has given, an enormous order for ammunition. Yet there is something behind that little conference, if only we could probe it, more interesting than you would believe, my friend.'

She paused. He waited eagerly, but she was silent for an unusually long time.

'You were suggesting,' he ventured to remind her, 'a few minutes ago, that there was some way in which intervention——'

She leaned a little towards him. Her hand rested for a second upon his.

'I have come to the conclusion,' she said, speaking very softly, 'that one of us, either you or I, must kill Ossendorf.'

He began to laugh and then stopped suddenly. A little shiver ran through him. For a single second her face was almost the face of a tigress. He felt that his laugh was a mistake.

'You are in earnest!' he muttered.

She rose from the table, gathered up her belongings and allowed him to arrange her cloak about her shoulders.

'Except that I retract that possible alternative,' she said calmly. 'I shall deal with Ossendorf myself.'

'But I don't understand,' he persisted.

'How should you?' she answered, smiling.

'By the by, where are we going? We spoke of a music hall, didn't we?'

'I have a box at the Empire,' he told her.

She was stepping by him into the taxi when she suddenly paused. Her frame seemed to become rigid.

'The Empire,' he told the driver.

She turned suddenly around.

'Your rooms,' she directed. 'Tell him to drive at once to your rooms.'

He was startled, but he obeyed her without hesitation. A moment later he took his place by her side.

'That valet of yours!' she exclaimed.

'What about him?'

'I told you that I knew his face. I have just remembered.'

'Well?'

'A year ago he was an attaché at the Japanese Embassy. His name is Baron Komashi.'

Lavendale was mystified.

'Are you sure?' he asked incredulously.

'Perfectly certain,' she insisted.

'But why on earth should he be a friend of Perkins and willing to act as my valet?'

'It's the eternal game,' she declared, 'and they are clever at it, too, the Japs. Tell me, have you any papers of special value about just now?'

'Yes, in my safe,' he admitted, 'but no one else has an idea of the combination.'

'Combination!' she scoffed. 'Niko Komashi, too! Tell me, are these papers political which you have inside that safe?'

'In a measure, yes!' he assented.

They had reached the street in which his rooms were situated.

'There is no light in my room,' he said, as they ascended the stairs. 'Niko must have done his work and gone home.'

'Yes,' she murmured, 'he has done his work, without a doubt. He has a knack of doing that.'

Lavendale produced his latch-key. The rooms appeared to be empty and in darkness. In the sitting-room he unlocked his safe and peered in. One by one he examined his papers. Everything was in perfect order. He turned back to his companion.

'Nothing has been disturbed,' he announced confidently.

She came over towards him, put her head for a moment inside the safe and immediately withdrew it.

'Niko has been through these papers during your absence,' she declared. 'If everything is there, it is because he had no need to steal. He has examined or made copies of what he chose.'

'How do you know this?' he asked incredulously.

'It is quite simple,' she explained. Even the cleverest man in the world seems always to forget one thing. Niko forgot that his clothes and fingers, even his breath, have always that peculiar Oriental perfume. What is it like—half almond-blossom, half sandalwood?'

'I remember I noticed it when he came in,' Lavendale agreed quickly.

'Put your head inside that safe again,' she directed.

He obeyed at once. When he emerged, his face was troubled. He locked the door mechanically.

'You are right,' he said.

They were silent for a moment. Lavendale was contemplating the lock in a dazed manner. He turned to Suzanne. She had seated herself in his easy-chair and had thrown back her cloak.

'You were going to tell me,' he reminded her, 'about this fellow Niko. You had an idea about him.'

'Mine is no idea,' she replied. 'It is a certainty. The man who posed this evening as your temporary valet, the man who in your absence has opened your safe, why, it is Baron Niko Komashi. He belongs to one of the most aristocratic families of Japan.'

'But he is a member of the Servants' Club!' Lavendale expostulated. 'He was a friend of Perkins—my servant!'

'Ostensibly,' she said dryly. 'He came over here as first secretary to the Embassy. Then he disappeared. No one quite knew what had become of him. I once had a suspicion. Now I know. You and I, my friend, are bunglers at the game he plays.'

Once more Lavendale was looking at the lock—unscratched, bearing so signs of having been tampered with.

'The thing is a miracle,' he muttered.

'Tell me—unless you would rather not,' she asked, leaning a little forward, 'was there any document in that safe likely to be of particular interest to the Japanese Secret Service?'

Lavendale's face was dark with mingled shame and humiliation.

'There was just the one document that should have been kept from them at all costs,' he declared bitterly. 'Two years ago I wrote a series of articles for an American Sunday paper upon our military unpreparedness. I don't know that they did any particular good, but, anyway, it's a subject I have studied closely. That paper I had my fingers on just now contains every possible scrap of information as to our standing army, our volunteer forces, our artillery, our possible scheme of defence on the west and the east, our stock of munitions, and our expenditure of same per thousand men. There was also an air and naval report and a scheme for mining San Francisco Harbour.'

She leaned back in her chair and laughed.

'Most interesting! I can quite understand how Niko's eyes would gleam! ... What's that?'

She turned her head suddenly. Lavendale, too, had started, and with a swift movement forward had touched the switch and plunged the room into darkness. They heard the soft click of the latch and the opening and closing of the front door. They heard the soft footsteps of the intruder across the hall. The door of the room in which they were was quietly opened and closed. Still with that same amazing stealthiness, a small, dark figure crossed the room and stood before the safe. Then there was a pause, several breathless moments of silence. Niko's instinct was telling him that he was not alone. Once more Lavendale's finger touched the switch and the lights blazed out. Niko was standing, the knob of the safe in his hand, his head turned towards them.

The sudden light had a common effect upon all of them. Suzanne for a moment held her hand in front of her eyes. Niko blinked slightly. Then he drew himself up to his full height of five feet four. He stood in front of the safe with his eyes fixed upon Lavendale, something about his face and attitude bearing a curious resemblance to a statue carved in wax. Lavendale coughed.

'You remind me, Baron Komashi,' he said, 'of an old English proverb—the pitcher that goes once too often to the well, you know. Was it something you had forgotten that brought you back? No, stay where you are, please.'

Niko remained motionless. Lavendale moved to a long, open cupboard which stood against the wall, opened it and groped about amongst its contents for a moment. Then he swung the door to and slipped some cartridges into the little revolver which he had taken from the top shelf. Niko's muscles suddenly seemed to relax. Ever so slightly he shrugged his shoulders. It was the gesture of a supreme philosophy.

'There's no need for a row,' Lavendale went on. 'The game you and I are playing at, Baron Komashi, requires finesse rather than muscle. By a stroke of genius you have read a certain document in that safe. That document is naturally of interest to the representative of the one country with whom America might possibly quarrel.'

Niko bowed his sleek head.

'I have read the document,' he confessed. 'It was my business here to read it. And now?'

'There you have me,' Lavendale admitted. 'It is a document, without a doubt, of great interest to you, and your Government will highly appreciate a résumé of its contents. At the same time, the only way to stop your making use of your information is to kill you.'

The man's face was like the face of a sphinx. Suzanne leaned a little further back in her chair and crossed her legs.

'It is a fortunate century in which you pursue your career, Baron,' she observed, 'and perhaps a fortunate country. These little qualms about human life which I can clearly see are influencing Mr. Lavendale, scarcely exist, even now, amongst your people, do they?'

'We are as yet,' Niko replied suavely, 'free, I am thankful to say, from the cowardice of the west.'

'If I asked you for your word of honour,' Lavendale continued, 'that you would not use that information?

'I might give it you,' Niko acknowledged, 'but my country's service is a higher thing than my personal honour, therefore it would do you no good. I shall be frank with you. There is no way you can prevent my report being duly made except by killing me. I am here, a self-confessed robber. If I were in your place, I should shoot.'

'The cowardice of the west, you see,' Lavendale remarked, throwing his revolver upon the table. 'You had better get out of the room. I might change my mind.'

For a moment Niko made no movement. Suzanne rose to her feet and lit a cigarette.

'As a matter of curiosity,' she asked, 'tell us why you returned, Baron?'

He bowed.

'The Empire performance is not over until half-past eleven,' he explained, 'and it is barely ten o'clock. I had some faint misgivings as to the resetting of the lock. I came back to examine it. That is my answer. You speak now of curiosity. I, too, have curiosity. Will you tell me how you knew that I had opened the safe?'

She smiled and lifted her handkerchief for a moment to her lips. Niko's head was bent as though in humiliation.

'It is so hard to outgrow one's errors,' he sighed.

He looked towards Lavendale and Lavendale pointed impatiently towards the door. He took a step or two in that direction, then he paused.

'Sir,' he said, looking back, 'because your methods are not mine, believe me that I still can appreciate their mistaken chivalry. The information I have gained I shall use. No promise of mine to the contrary would avail you. But there is, perhaps, some return which I might offer, more valuable, perhaps, to mademoiselle, yet of some import to you also.'

Suzanne leaned a little forward. Her cigarette burnt idly between her fingers.

'In this great conflict,' Niko continued, 'whose reverberations shake the earth, Japan watches from afar off. There are few who know the reason, but there is a reason. Let that pass. My country lays no seal upon my lips. What I know I pass on to you. A hundred million cartridges and five thousand tons of heavier ammunition, which might otherwise have reached Russia, are lying now at the bottom of the ocean. This is the doing of one man, a man in the pay of Germany, a man who is the greatest traitor the world has ever known.'

'Ossendorf!' Suzanne cried.

Niko bowed and moved towards the door.

'Mademoiselle has suspected, perhaps,' he concluded. 'It is I who can assure her that her suspicions are just. The greatest plant in America is kept producing munitions by day and night, bought with Russian gold but never meant to reach their destination. It is well?'

He looked at Lavendale, his hand upon the door. Lavendale nodded curtly.

'It is well,' he said.

*****

Mr. Jacob P. Weald smoothed out the document which he had been examining and drew a deep sigh of satisfaction.

'Say, Ed,' he remarked, turning to his secretary, who was smoking a cigar at the other end of the room, 'that's worth a cool million apiece for us, that contract.'

'Hope there's no hitch,' the other replied anxiously. 'What's this young fellow from the Embassy want?'

'Nothing to hurt us,' Weald assured him. 'We're all right with the authorities all round. I'm glad, Ed, we did the square thing. We've had it straight from the British War Office to go right along ahead and give Russia everything we can turn out. Well, Russia's going to have it, and, by gum, there's enough ammunition provided for in that contract to make mincemeat of the whole German Army!'

There was a knock at the door of the sitting-room and a servant announced Mr. Ambrose Lavendale. Lavendale, following closely behind, shook hands at once with the two men.

'I've heard of your plant, Mr. Weald,' he said pleasantly. 'Wonderful things you've been doing in the way of producing ammunition, they tell me. Been unlucky some with your shipments, though, haven't you?'

'That's so,' the other admitted, 'but that's not our fault. We don't come in there. Our friends have their own steamships, eleven of them, bought for the job.'

'Lost two out of three already, haven't they?' Lavendale remarked.

'Say, you seem some wise, young man,' Mr. Weald said pleasantly. 'However, I got the note from the boss. What can we do for you?'

'A very small thing,' Lavendale replied. 'I understand that Baron Ossendorf is coming here to sign that contract at twelve o'clock.'

'You're dead right, sir,' Mr. Weald admitted, 'and there's a magnum of the best standing there in the ice, waiting for the psychological moment.'

'Mind my being present and asking him one question—just one?' Lavendale inquired.

'We ain't likely to object to anything you want to do, young fellow,' Mr. Weald assured him. 'Ed Jenkins there—he's secretary of the company—and I, have got no crooked ideas about this business. We are going to bring a few million dollars into our own pockets, but we are going to do it on the straight. What our Ambassador over here says, goes, and his note asks us to take you into this.'

There was a knock at the door. Ossendorf was announced and promptly entered. He held out a hand each to Weald and Jenkins. Then he glanced inquiringly at Lavendale.

'This is a young friend of ours from the American Embassy,' Mr. Weald explained. 'Mr. Ambrose Lavendale—Baron Ossendorf. He's a kind of witness that all's right and above-board.'

Baron Ossendorf bowed and held out his long, elegantly-shaped hand.

'I am delighted, Mr. Lavendale,' he said, 'delighted that you should be a participator in our little business this morning. Between Russia and America there have always been the most cordial sentiments of friendship. It is a pleasure to us to think that we are able, at these terrible times, to be of service to one another.... You have the contract, Mr. Weald? Ah!' he added, glancing at it through his eyeglass, 'I see that this is the draft which I have already perused. Nothing remains, then, but for me to sign it.'

He dipped his pen in the ink, stooped down and there was a moment's silence whilst his pen spluttered across the paper. Mr. Weald began to cut the strings of the magnum of champagne.

'Just one moment,' Lavendale interposed. 'There is a little condition, Baron, which it is not proposed to put officially into the agreement, a very small matter, but may I suggest it to you?'

Ossendorf turned his head. His eyes had narrowed a little.

'By all means, sir.'

'The contract,' Lavendale continued slowly, 'is for the whole production of the Weald Plant for six months, with option of continuance until the end of the war. Shipments are to be made weekly by steamers whose names are given there, steamers practically acquired by the Russian Government.'

'You are well informed, my young friend,' Ossendorf admitted quietly.

'It has been suggested,' Lavendale said, speaking slowly and looking Ossendorf in the face, 'that you should change the wireless operator on all those vessels for a person approved by the British Government.'

There was a moment's deep silence. Mr. Weald had paused with his knife already pressed against the last string of the bottle. Jenkins was standing with his mouth open, a little dazed. Ossendorf shrank back as though he had received a blow. It was obvious that he retained his composure with an effort.

'What do you mean?' he demanded.

'Simply this,' Lavendale replied firmly. 'Already the *Iris* and the *Southern Star*, with enough ammunition on board to have supplied an army, have gone to the bottom. I mean, sir, that every one of those remaining nine boats on which is to be packed the whole production of the greatest ammunition plant in America, is doomed to go to the bottom.'

Two great drops of sweat had broken out on Ossendorf's forehead. His face seemed suddenly to have grown thinner. His mouth was open. He glared at Lavendale, but he was utterly incapable of speech. The latter turned to Weald.

'Mr. Weald,' he said, 'this contract for your entire output can be signed within twenty-four hours, either by a representative of Russia other than Baron Ossendorf, or by the secretary of the British Munition Board. This man Ossendorf is a paid traitor—the Judas of the war.'

Mr. Weald was incapable of coherent speech.

'You mean,' Jenkins faltered, 'that he is in the pay of Germany?'

'Ask him!' Lavendale suggested scornfully.

Ossendorf seemed to wither up. He staggered to his feet and groped to the door. Suddenly something flashed in his hands, clasped tightly between them. There was a loud report, the room seemed filled with smoke. They all three looked in a dazed manner at the figure stretched upon the carpet, face downwards, the shoulders still twitching slightly. Lavendale stood with his finger upon the bell.

'Sorry to have interfered, Mr. Weald,' he said, 'but your stuff's wanted somewhere else—not at the bottom of the sea.' ...

Ossendorf's body was carried away. It was very well understood that the matter was to be hushed up. Lavendale lingered with Mr. Weald, who was walking restlessly about the room, still scarcely able to realize what had happened.

'Poor devil!' he kept on muttering. 'Poor devil!'

Lavendale laid his hand firmly upon his compatriot's shoulder.

'Look here, Mr. Weald,' he said, 'there are good and bad of every nation—Germans, Americans, English, or French. This man was outside the pale. He was a black and dastardly traitor, the pariah of humanity, he trafficked with the lives of human beings, he was a murderer for gold. If anything, his end was too merciful.'

Mr. Weald nodded reflectively. Lavendale's words were convincing. His eyes wandered towards the champagne bottle upon the sideboard. He was feeling the strain.

'In that case,' he murmured, 'perhaps——'

CHAPTER IV.
GENERAL MATRAVERS REPAYS

Mademoiselle Suzanne de Freyne was travelling back to England in hot haste. On the French train she received courtesies rarely extended in these days to any solitary passenger, and at Boulogne she was hurried from the gangway of the steamer back on to the dock and into an evil-looking, four-funnelled British destroyer. Almost as she set foot on board, they moved away from the landing-stage. An officer came forward to meet her and saluted.

'The Captain's cabin is at your disposal, Miss de Freyne,' he announced. 'We have an invalided General on board, but we've tucked him up in a bunk. Afraid we shall give you a bit of a shaking up.'

'I am a very good sailor,' Suzanne assured him. 'It is delightful that I am able to come across with you. Time counts for so much, these days.'

'We haven't any stewardess,' the young officer remarked, as he threw open the door of the cabin. 'You'll ring the bell for anything you want, though. Parsons is an awfully good fellow. And you'll excuse me, won't you? I'm on duty.'

He hurried up on deck, and in a few moments the destroyer was clear of the harbour and tearing across the Channel into the sombre blackness of the night. Huge waves, with a thunderous roar, swept her decks. The spray leapt high above the tops of her squat funnels, from which flashed little jets of flame. Suzanne, driven from the cabin by the craving for air, stood half-way up the companion-way, looking into the blackness. Here and there, a star seemed to reel across the face of the sky and more than once a cloud of spray swept over her head. Unhesitatingly, as though driven by some superhuman hand, they ploughed their way through the black wall of space to their destination. After the turmoil of the Channel, their slow gliding up to the side of the dock seemed almost ghostlike. Suzanne felt almost as though she herself were breathless as she stood at last upon the soaking deck. There were a couple of dim lights and a few shadowy figures upon the quay. The young officer who had spoken to her at Boulogne, stood by her side.

'We are throwing a gangway across for you, Miss de Freyne. I'm afraid we gave you rather a rough crossing.'

'I do not mind it,' she declared. 'I was only anxious to come quickly. Do you know if I shall be able to get on to London at once?'

'There will be a special for the General,' he told her. 'They'll probably take you, too.'

The gangway was thrown across. The young man saluted, and Suzanne stepped on to the rain-sodden dock. An official stepped up to her at once.

'Miss de Freyne?' he inquired.

'Yes?'

'There is a special waiting here for General Matravers. I have had instructions to attach a coach for you.'

'That is very delightful!' she exclaimed. 'Shall I follow you?'

The man piloted her across the track and handed her into an ordinary first-class compartment attached to the waiting train.

'Sorry we've had to give the saloon to General Matravers,' he explained. 'Will you have any tea or coffee, or anything to eat?'

She gave an order to the refreshment boy whom he summoned, and threw herself down with a sigh of content into the corner seat. Presently a tall man in khaki, with his arm in a sling and leaning upon a stick, came up the platform, followed by two junior officers. He was shown at once into the saloon and a little murmur of animated conversation arose. Five minutes later the train glided away, leaving the two junior officers disconsolate upon the long, wooden platform; passed through the two stations, and, gathering speed at every moment, rushed away northwards.

Suzanne had more than once boasted that she had no nerves. She finished her coffee and sandwiches, lit a cigarette and curled herself up in her corner. For a few moments she looked out into the darkness, watching the scanty lights. Then her eyes turned, entirely by chance, towards the door which connected her carriage with the saloon. They had no sooner rested upon it than a queer, inexplicable sense of uneasiness crept over her. She tried to look away from it, to look out of the opposite window, to interest herself in the evening paper. She read a line or two, then found herself slowly lowering the sheet, found herself peering over the top towards that closed door of dark red mahogany with its brass handle. She threw the paper down, walked to the end of the carriage and back again. She must be going mad, she told herself. The only occupant of that saloon was a wounded soldier of great distinction, a General whose deeds in the earlier stages of the war had made history. He was alone there without even an A.D.C., and in any case the door was probably locked. What cause of uneasiness for her could there be in his proximity? She fought against her fit of nerves valiantly, but she found herself tearing the paper into small pieces, crumbling the remains of her roll between her fingers, sipping desperately the remnants of her cold coffee. And all the time her eyes seemed glued upon that brass door-knob. If it should move! She set her teeth to keep from screaming. When the thing really happened, it seemed to bring, to a certain extent, release from her hysterical fears. Yet for the first few seconds it paralyzed her. The handle turned, slowly and deliberately. The door was pushed open towards her. A man looked in, stooping by reason of his height, a lean, gaunt man clad in the uniform of a General. He looked at her for a moment without speech. Then he came into the compartment and closed the door behind him.

'What do you want?' she asked hoarsely.

He saluted mechanically.

'I am General Matravers,' he announced. 'May I sit down?'

She glanced at the communication cord—it was on the distant side of the carriage. Why she should have been afraid of him she could not tell, yet she felt as though she had never been in such danger in her life as when he took the seat opposite to her.

'I am General Matravers,' he repeated. 'You have heard of me, perhaps?'

'But naturally,' she assented. 'We have all read of your wonderful exploits at Mons.'

He moistened his lips with his tongue. His face seemed curiously dried up, his eyes were hard, his features grim and bony. He presented somehow a queer impression of lifelessness.

'Mons!' he muttered ruminatingly. 'You've never been to Hell, have you, young lady?'

'Not yet,' she answered, watching him closely.

'That was the beginning of it,' he went on. 'We need a Dante, young lady, to sing to us of those days, when the winds were driven from the face of the earth by the screeching of the shells and the roar and the clash of the guns, and they seemed to be always nearer.... Every foot of ground was red with blood, the blood of our dear soldiers, and one thought of the people at home.... I know men who lost their reason at Mons.'

'It must have been terrible,' she faltered.

He sat opposite to her, nervously opening and closing the interlocked fingers of his hands.

'You know why I am coming home?' he asked abruptly. 'Medals enough here, you see, for a field-marshal, and I am sent home in disgrace.'

She murmured something to which he paid no attention whatever.

'I left my two A.D.C.'s at Folkestone,' he went on, 'forbade them to enter the train. They are worried about me. Perhaps they are right. You see, it was at—but we don't mention names—my headquarters last week. It was the night before our advance. You read about that. I won't mention the name of the place. We called it a partial success. But for the thing I am going to tell you, it might have been the turning point of the war. The attack failed—my fault.'

'I read that your division did splendidly,' she remarked.

Again he moistened his dry lips. His hands were shaking now by his side; he seemed like a man on the verge of paralysis.

'This is what happened,' he continued. 'I was at headquarters, my own headquarters. My orderly reported a Staff Officer from the French headquarters. He came in, a typical-looking young French soldier, wearing the uniform of one of their best regiments, one of those which I knew were in the division which was to join up with ours in the morning. He was tall and dark, with a thin, black moustache, long, narrow eyes, a scar on his right cheek, sallow, and with a queer habit of swinging his left arm. He brought me some intelligible, perfectly coherent verbal instructions, asked a few questions as to my plans for the next day, gave me a personal message from the French General commanding the division, saluted, got back into his motor-car and drove off. And I thought no more about it until we found out that our whole scheme of attack was known to the enemy, and that they were prepared for us at every point. He was a German. We were sold. Thousands of my men were lost through that. My fault. He was a German. Are you a German, young lady?'

'Ah, but no!' she exclaimed, shrinking a little back.

'You are not wholly English.'

'I am half French and half English,' she told him.

'The French are good people,' he went on, relapsing into his former far-away tone, 'very fine people. They can fight too, and they can tell Germans when they see them. That is why I am going home—because I couldn't. I've sworn that the next German I see, I'll kill. You're not a German, are you?'

'I told you just now,' she reminded him quietly, 'that I am half French and half English—mostly French. I am in the service of the French Government at the present moment, trying to help you, General.'

'Good girl,' he said absently. 'I thought there might have been a German in here when I heard some one moving. If I can't find one, I suppose I must shoot myself.'

He took out a little revolver and examined it. He opened the breech and she saw that it was fully loaded.

'May I look?' she asked.

He handed it to her at once. The window by which they sat was half down. She calmly threw it out. He looked at her in a mildly-vexed manner.

'You should not have done that, young lady,' he expostulated. 'I was very fond of that revolver. Besides, how am I to kill myself now?'

'I should wait,' she advised him. 'When you get to London you will easily find Germans—too many of them.'

He shook his head.

'But I've nothing to kill them with, and I've left my army behind. I am sent home,' he added, with a sudden hoarse pathos.

Her sense of personal fear had passed. She knew that the dangerous moment, if indeed there had been one, lay behind.

'There is so much work to be done in England,' she said.

He seemed to be looking through the carriage windows; his hands were twitching horribly.

'Those nights,' he muttered, 'when we thought that an hour's rest had come, and the red fires came spitting from our flanks just when we thought ourselves safe, when we thought them far and away behind——'

His words became unintelligible. He sat quite quiet. Presently, to her joy, she saw a carpet of lights on either side and knew that they were running into London.

'You had better get back to your saloon,' she said. 'We shall be at Charing Cross in a few minutes, and there will probably be some one to meet you.'

He rose obediently to his feet. The tears were in her eyes as he turned away with a stiff little salute, and, stooping low, disappeared through the doorway. Then she leaned back with a long-drawn sigh of relief. It was a strange little episode, another of the little adventures which gave colour to her life. She leaned out of the window and saw the last of him as they drew up. He was met by an officer and an elderly lady. She saw him pass out and take his place in a waiting motor-car. Then she stepped out herself, handed her bag to a porter and was conducted to a taxicab.

*****

Suzanne sat, the next afternoon, under the trees at Ranelagh with Lavendale. She leaned back in her chair and breathed a little sigh of contentment.

'And you, my friend,' she asked, 'what have you been doing?'

'Nothing,' he answered. I am waiting for a man to arrive from America. His coming, I fancy, will provide me with work, but until then there is nothing for me. To pass the time while you were in France, I went over to Holland last week.'

She nodded.

'The one country left which may provide us with a sensation,' she remarked. 'I suppose that is why you went.'

'I made a few inquiries,' he replied. 'My own impression of the people was that they wanted peace very badly and Schnapps more than anything else in the world.'

She laughed softly. It was significant of his attitude towards her that he asked no questions of her own doings.

'I had a curious adventure on my way back from Paris yesterday,' she told him. 'I travelled up from Boulogne in a special with General Matravers.'

'Matravers?' he repeated. 'Isn't he one of the British Generals who have been sent home?'

'I believe so,' she assented, 'in fact I am sure of it. He told me the whole story on the way up. Afterwards he brought out a revolver and swore that he was going to shoot himself.'

'What on earth did you do?' he exclaimed.

'I took it away from him,' she replied. 'He wasn't in the least dangerous, really.'

'Look here,' Lavendale declared earnestly, 'I think it's quite time you left off this travelling about alone.'

She laughed gaily.

'But, my friend,' she protested, 'what would you have? Can a trusted agent'—she glanced around for a moment and lowered her voice—'of the French and English Secret Service engage a chaperon?'

'I don't care,' he answered, a little doggedly. 'It's all very well for us men to take a risk or two, but it's no sort of life for a girl——'

She checked him at once.

'You don't understand,' she interrupted. 'I am a daughter of France. Every drop of blood in my body, every part of myself, my soul, even, belongs to my country. The work I am doing I shall go on with, whatever it might cost me.'

He did not attempt to argue with her, the finality of her tone was too absolute.

'I suppose it is because of this spirit,' he said, 'that France is invincible. Tell me——'

He broke off in his sentence. Her fingers had suddenly gripped his arm, she had leaned forward in her place. Coming down the steps on to the terrace was a little group of soldiers in staff uniform. One of them, in the centre of the group, was obviously a foreigner, and, from the respect with which they all treated him, a person of distinction.

'Who are they?' she asked.

'I expect they are members of the military mission from France,' he explained. 'They are being entertained down here to dinner to-night by some officials from the War Office. The head-waiter told me about it. I tackled him about a table in case you cared to stay down.'

'But only one of them is a foreigner,' she observed.

He shrugged his shoulders.

'I really don't know anything more about it,' he said. 'I don't suppose any one does. Why are you so interested?'

She said nothing for a moment. The Frenchman was standing chatting amiably in the centre of the terrace, and Suzanne watched him with curious intensity. He was tall, he had a slight black moustache, his eyes were long and narrow, there was a scar on his right cheek. He was the very prototype of the man who had arisen in her mind a few hours ago, called into being by those hoarse, broken-hearted words of the ruined General.

'I must know his name,' she insisted.

He looked at her wonderingly.

'But, my dear——'

'I must know his name,' she repeated. 'Please help me. Don't ask me why.'

He rose at once.

'I'll do my best,' he promised her.

He disappeared into the house. The little party of men strolled backwards and forwards along the terrace. In about five minutes Lavendale reappeared. He smiled as he approached.

'I got hold of the dinner cards,' he announced in triumph. 'His name is Lieutenant-Colonel Leychelles.'

The little company of soldiers at that moment began to descend the steps. Suzanne rose to her feet and, standing under the shadow of the trees, she leaned forward. The man whom she had been watching with so much interest, was distinctly swinging his left arm. She gripped Lavendale by the elbow.

'Come with me,' she insisted. 'Come with me at once. Take me up to town.'

He obeyed promptly. They passed through the house and Lavendale ordered up his car.

'Where to?' he asked, as he took his place at the driving wheel.

'I must find General Matravers,' she declared. 'Drive up towards London. I must think as we go.'

They glided down the drive, over Hammersmith Bridge and up to the Park.

'Don't you belong to a club somewhere?' she asked. 'We must get a Who's Who.'

'Why, of course,' he answered. 'We can manage that easily enough.'

He pulled up presently outside the door of the Bath Club in Dover Street.

'If you'll wait here for half a moment,' he suggested.

She nodded and he sprang down and ran lightly up the steps. He was back again almost at once.

'The first name I came across,' he announced,—'17 Belgrave Square is the town address. Shall I drive there? It's quite close.'

She assented. In a few moments they arrived at their destination. Suzanne stood under the stone portico and rang the bell. In due course a butler appeared.

'General Matravers is not seeing anybody, madam,' was his prompt reply to Suzanne's inquiry. 'The doctor has ordered him complete rest.'

'My business,' Suzanne explained, 'is very urgent.'

'So every reporter who has been here to-day has told me,' the man replied a little wearily. No one has been allowed to see him.'

'Is Lady Matravers in?' Suzanne persisted.

'Lady Matravers is not receiving. Perhaps you would like to leave your name and a message, madam?' the man suggested.

A tall, dark-haired woman, who had been crossing the hall, paused. She came a few steps towards Suzanne.

'I am Lady Matravers,' she announced, 'Can I do anything for you?'

Suzanne pressed forward and the butler stood on one side.

'Lady Matravers,' the former said earnestly, I have the most important business with your husband. I know he is ill—I came up from Folkestone with him yesterday—and yet I must see him.'

'You were his companion in the special train?' Lady Matravers asked. 'He spoke of a young lady who travelled up with him.'

'I am the young lady,' Suzanne assented. 'I am in the Secret Service of France,' she went on, dropping her voice a little. 'Your husband told me some curious things last night. It is in connection with one of them that I wish to see him. It isn't for my own sake, Lady Matravers. It is for the sake of the country.'

The door was thrown open. General Matravers, leaning upon his stick, came into the hall. He was looking very white and shaken, but he seemed to recognize Suzanne. He looked at her doubtfully.

'It is the young lady whom I found last night in the carriage attached to my saloon,' he remarked, 'the young lady, my dear,' he added, turning to his wife, 'who threw my revolver out of the window.'

Lady Matravers glanced towards the servant who was lingering in the background and led Suzanne back into the room from which she herself had issued. The General followed her. A quiet-faced woman in nurse's uniform rose from a chair as they entered.

'If you are really the young lady who travelled with my husband from Folkestone last night,' Lady Matravers said kindly, 'I am very glad indeed to meet you. He has told me such very nice things about you. The doctor's orders are that he is not to be disturbed on any account, but if you wish to speak to him for a few minutes, here he is. I was just trying to persuade him to go to bed when you came.'

'Perhaps what I have come to say may do your husband more good than harm,' Suzanne assured her. 'General,' she added, turning towards him, 'do you mind describing to me once more the man who came to your headquarters masquerading as a French officer, an envoy from the French Brigadier-General?'

The General's face darkened.

'Describe him!' he exclaimed. 'Why, I can't get him out of my thoughts for a minute! He was tall, soldierly, dark, sallow, black moustache, narrow eyes, black hair cut short, a scar on his right cheek, and he had a habit swinging his left arm when he walked.'

'I need not ask you whether you would know him again,' Suzanne said, 'because I am sure you would. I may be very foolish and I may be making a very silly mistake, but there is a man over here now attached to the French Military Mission. He is being entertained to-night at Ranelagh by officials from the War Office. He leaves to-morrow, ostensibly for French headquarters, and he answers your description exactly.'

All the nervousness had left the General's manner. He was perfectly calm, a little eager. He picked up his cap and cane from a table.

'Where is he to be found?' he asked.

'If you will come with me,' Suzanne promised, 'I will take you to him.'

The nurse hastened towards them. The General pushed her aside. His tone had acquired a new firmness.

'Please understand, both of you,' he said, 'that no nurse or doctor's injunctions will keep me from doing my duty. My dear,' he added, turning to his wife and kissing her upon the forehead, 'this is not a matter in which you must interfere. If the young lady is mistaken, I shall come back at once. If by any chance she is right, it is imperative that I should go. I am at your service, madam.'

'I will take care of him,' Suzanne whispered to Lady Matravers.

They let him go, doubtfully but of compulsion. He took his place in the car and acknowledged his introduction to Lavendale with a stiff salute. They started off at once. For the first time Suzanne began to be a little nervous about the outcome of their journey.

'This man,' she explained, 'is being entertained at dinner at Ranelagh at the present moment. We can go down there and you can see from the open doorway of the dining-room whether there is any truth in my suspicions. If we are wrong— —'

'You need have no fear, young lady,' the General assured her calmly. 'I am a member of Ranelagh and well-known there. It will be quite in order that I stroll round the place and glance in at the dining-room. If your suspicions are, as you suggest, ill-founded, no harm will be done. If they are true,' he added, his voice shaking for a moment, 'if really it is vouchsafed to me in this life to find myself face to face once more with that man——'

He broke off abruptly and muttered something under his breath. Not another word was spoken until they had turned in at the avenue and pulled up in front of the clubhouse. The General had become preternaturally calm. He waited, however, for Suzanne to precede him.

'If you will lead the way, young lady,' he suggested.

They crossed through the two rooms, out on to the terrace the other side, and turned towards the dining-room. The gardens were bright with flowers, and the glow of the sunset seemed still to linger about the place. One or two visitors who had dined early were already having their coffee under the trees. From a hidden spot the musicians were tuning their instruments. Suzanne felt her heart beat rapidly as they drew near the dining-room; the General, apparently unmoved, walked with measured tread, a commanding and dignified figure. A couple of young soldiers stood up as he passed, and he accepted their salute genially. Then he passed into the dining-room. Almost immediately in front of him, at the table usually reserved for the golfers' luncheon, the dinner-party was proceeding, and on the right-hand side of the host sat the distinguished Frenchman. He was facing the door and he glanced up at the entrance of the little party. Suzanne asked no questions. She felt her breath almost stop, a little sob choked her. The faces of almost every one in the room, the laughter, the murmur of conversation, seemed suddenly in her mind to have become arrested. More than anything else in the world she was conscious of this one thing—the man who sat there knew that his hour had come, knew that Fate was marching towards him in the shape of that grim, military figure.

The General walked towards the party very much with the air of one who had come to make some casual inquiry. It was only when he was recognized that a little interested murmur stole around the room.

He walked to within a few feet of the Frenchman and his right hand seemed to have disappeared for a moment.

'Gentlemen,' he said, without unduly raising his voice but with curious distinctness, 'the man whom you are entertaining here as an emissary from our French allies, is an impostor, a German and a spy. He cost me, a few weeks ago, the lives of two thousand of my men. A far smaller thing, he is responsible for the ruin of my reputation. This is less than he deserves.'

With hand as steady as a rock, the General held his revolver out before him and deliberately fired three times at the man whom he had accused, and who had fallen forward now, his outstretched hands sweeping the wineglasses from in front of him—stone dead. The General watched his victim without emotion. He even leaned forward to make sure that the wounds were mortal. Then he walked deliberately out into the garden, heedless of the shrieking of the women, the crowd of diners who had sprung to their feet, the passing of the paralysis which had seemed to keep every one in the room seated and silent.

*****

They found the proofs upon his body that night—horrifying, stupefying proofs—and the censor's hand came down. No word of that tragedy ever appeared under any sensational headline in any newspaper. In the face of that grim silence, even many of those who had been present found themselves wondering whether that lightning tragedy had not been a nightmare of the brain. To Suzanne de Freyne, however, it remained always one of the tense moments of her life. The General, with the revolver still in his hand, turned towards her with a polite gesture and a happy smile as he led the way into the garden. He tossed the weapon into a bed of geraniums and seemed utterly indifferent to the turmoil around.

'You were right, young lady,' he said. 'That was the man.'

CHAPTER V.
SUSCEPTIBLE MR. KESSNER

There was a vigour in her walk, a determination in her face, which made Lavendale pause for an instant before he crossed the street to accost Suzanne de Freyne. It was perfectly clear to him that she was bound upon a serious errand. She was dressed with her usual subdued elegance but with more, even, than her usual simplicity. In her black tailor-made costume, her small hat and neat patent shoes, she looked like the Rue de la Paix at four o'clock in the afternoon during its halcyon days. He was forced to quicken his pace to intercept her.

'Good morning, Miss de Freyne!'

She turned quickly around and held out her left hand. Her greeting was cordial enough, but her air of abstraction did not altogether disappear.

'Where have you been hiding for the last few days?' she asked.

'I came back from Holland last night,' he replied. 'I have been in Germany again.'

'Any news?' she asked quickly.

'Nothing very wonderful. I needn't ask how things are with you. I can tell that you have something on hand. Can I help?'

She laughed.

'You are right in a way, but I don't think you can help,' she told him. 'This is quite an important morning—it is Celia's sale.'

He was a little staggered. Her manner was convincing.

'You mean that you are going to a millinery sale?'

'Don't be silly,' she answered. 'The first morning of Celia's sale is the most important event of the season. We have printed cards of invitation, and policemen outside the door to keep away intruders. This isn't any ordinary bargain hunting, you know. This is our one chance to provide ourselves with the elegancies of life at a reasonable cost.'

'For the moment, I gather,' he went on, falling into step with her, 'the affairs of the nation are in the background.'

'Naturally,' she assented.

'At what hour,' he inquired, 'will this function be over?'

She glanced at him suspiciously.

'If I thought you were making fun— —'

'Never entered into my head,' he assured her.

'Then you can give me some lunch at one o'clock,' she promised.

'That's exactly what I was hoping for. And, Miss de Freyne?'

'Well?'

'Would you mind very much if I brought an acquaintance?'

She glanced at him in some surprise.

'Of course not,' she answered, 'only it must be a grill-room luncheon, please. I am dressed for a scrimmage.'

'At one o'clock at the Milan Grill,' he told her, raising his hat.

He strolled slowly away southwards, crossed Pall Mall, and let himself in by a side entrance to the American Embassy. Here he spent a few minutes in the outer offices and passed on, a little later, into a more private apartment. An elderly man with a clean-shaven face, grey hair brushed back from his forehead, and tortoiseshell-rimmed spectacles, looked up from his roll-topped desk and waved his visitor to a seat.

'Hullo, Ambrose! Anything fresh?'

Lavendale drew up a chair and grasped the hand which the other offered him.

'There is plenty going on, if one could get to understand it, Mr. Washburn,' he said. 'Berlin had me puzzled.'

'When did you get back?'

'Last night.'

'See anything of our friend?'

'He crossed with me.'

'Get acquainted with him?'

'Oh! I knew him before in Washington and in New York,' Lavendale replied. 'I took care to remind him of it, too. Yes, he was quite friendly. All the same, he was secretive. He didn't tell me the one thing I discovered of the greatest interest in connection with his trip, and that was that the Kaiser sent his private car three hundred miles and met him at the Western Headquarters. They spent the best part of the day together. Has he been in here?'

Mr. Washburn shook his head.

'He neither reported before he left, nor has he been in since he got back. Kind of giving us the cold shoulder, isn't it?'

'He hasn't had much time yet,' Lavendale remarked thoughtfully, 'but it certainly doesn't look exactly like the behaviour of a loyal American.'

Mr. Washburn turned in his place, removed his spectacles from his eyes and rubbed them carefully with his handkerchief. A slight weariness was apparent in his face and tone.

'That's our great trouble, Ambrose,' he said. 'Germany's a mighty country. She holds her sons in a closer grip than any other nation in the world. A German-American is a German first and an American afterwards, and don't you forget it. That's what makes us such a polyglot, indiscriminate race. Are you going to make a report?'

'Not at present,' Lavendale replied. 'I haven't yet pieced together the scraps I was able to pick up. Let it be for a day or two. What I am anxious to find out is whether Kessner reports here or not, and what account he gives, if any, of his journey to Germany.'

'I'll send you word directly he shows up, if he comes at all,' Mr. Washburn promised. 'I hear there are half-a-dozen more of his gang in London.'

Lavendale nodded.

'They've some sort of a show on. Kessner as good as admitted it to me.'

'Where do you stand with him?' Mr. Washburn asked curiously.

'I'm all right up to the present,' Lavendale asserted. 'He believes I went over on a mission about the British prisoners, 'and he's inclined to fancy I may be useful to him. Anyway, he is lunching with me today.'

Mr. Washburn smiled.

'If you think you'll get much out of him, young fellow,' he said, 'I fancy you're looking for disappointment. The brains that made twenty million in Wall Street and control an organization so secret that we can't even put a finger upon it——'

'Yes, I know,' Lavendale interrupted, rising, 'but, you know, there's always chance to be reckoned with, and I've one card up my sleeve, anyway. I know all about him and he doesn't suspect me yet.'

...

'Exactly why am I asked to this festive lunch?' Suzanne de Freyne inquired, as she leaned back upon a settee in the small lounge which led into the Milan grill-room, at a few minutes before one o'clock that morning.

'Because I am up against a cul-de-sac,' Lavendale confessed, 'and I want your woman's wit to show me the way out.'

'You seem to be taking it for granted that we are allies,' she remarked.

'We are to a certain extent,' he pleaded. 'You must admit that a Germanized United States would be bad for you, and that is what we have to fight against.'

A waiter set down two cocktails upon a small table in front of them. She sipped hers deliberately.

'Tell me, what is the trouble with this man Kessner?' she asked. 'Of what is it that you really suspect him?'

'I wish I knew,' Lavendale groaned. 'These are the bald facts. Washington and New York, during the last six months, have been the scene of the most desperate efforts of German diplomacy and political manoeuvring, with one sole aim—that of preventing the export of munitions of war to England or France. Money has been spent like water but the progress has been too slow. Germany has gained adherents to her point of view, but not enough. America is in a position to be of immense use to the Allies and none whatever to Germany or Austria, and up to the present she shows no signs of ceasing to supply England and France and Russia with all the munitions she can turn out. The German Party in America have taken stock of these things. They have measured their weakness and tasted defeat. Everything up to this point has been above-board. We understood perfectly well what they were fighting for, and to a certain extent admitted their grievance.'

'They had no grievance,' Miss de Freyne interposed.

'Perhaps not a logical one,' Lavendale admitted, 'but you see it is perfectly true that while they are supplying munitions on an immense scale to the Allies, they are supplying none at all to Germany and Austria. That is, of course, owing to England's control of the sea, but it is galling to Germany and Austria to know that a neutral country is providing her enemies with the means of waging warfare against her. From their point of view it is not ideal neutrality, is it?'

'America is perfectly ready to supply Germany and Austria as well,' she reminded him. 'Besides, Germany and Austria both supplied England during the Boer War.'

'That, of course, is what makes America's position logical,' he went on, 'but listen. Kessner and his friends have obviously come to an end of their intriguing in the direction of stopping supplies. They have dropped their newspaper campaign. They have shrugged their shoulders and apparently accepted the inevitable. No one who knows them would believe them capable of anything of the sort. Kessner has been over here for a month. He was in Germany when I was. He spent a week with the Chancellor and a long time with the Kaiser himself. Heyl and both the Hindemanns are over here, too. They have also been in Germany. You see, they are all entitled to call themselves Americans, although they are Germans at heart.'

'You think that there is some fresh scheme on?' she asked.

'I am perfectly certain there is,' he said firmly. 'Not only that, but I have an idea as to its bearing.... This is our friend. If you don't know him by sight, prepare for a shock.'

A small man, dressed in plain black clothes, with broad-toed shoes and a tie almost clerical in its simplicity, had entered the place and was handing his bowler hat to an attendant. His complexion was sallow, his general air one of complete insignificance. Suzanne watched the greeting between the two with intense interest. It was hard to realize that this was Ludwig Kessner, twenty times a millionaire.

The little man's speech and manners wholly belied his appearance. His assurance was unlimited. He talked easily and with confidence.

'Well, young fellow,' he exclaimed, 'so we are back in London, eh? Not late, am I?'

'Not a moment,' Lavendale assured him. 'I want to present you, if I may, to Miss de Freyne, who is lunching with us. Miss de Freyne,' he added, 'this is Mr. Kessner.'

She rose with a charming little smile and shook hands with him. Mr. Kessner seemed to see no reason why he should conceal his admiration. He walked close to her side as they entered the luncheon-room.

'Our young friend and I,' he remarked, 'were hanging over the side of a steamer, looking out for submarines, this time yesterday. Not particularly good for the appetite, that sort of thing.'

'I think it is very brave of you to have really crossed the North Sea,' Suzanne declared. 'I should have been terrified to death.'

'Business is business,' Mr. Kessner observed, 'and I am something of a fatalist myself. I go about what I have to do and take my chances. Same with Mr. Lavendale, I expect, only these diplomatists are used to it. Troublous times, Miss de Freyne, times such as I never dreamed we should see in our days. By the by, are you French or English?'

'French, English, and Austrian,' she told him, smiling, as they took their places at the table, 'so you see I represent neutrality in my own person. My grandmother was Austrian, and I have never been so happy as when I lived in Vienna.'

He nodded approvingly.

'Do you know,' he said, 'I am glad you are not altogether English. I don't know which way your sympathies may be in this trouble, and I don't know as it matters. We each of us have a right to our feelings, whatever they may be. I am an American first and foremost, like our friend here, only he has British blood in his veins behind it, and I have German. We can keep good friends for all that, though.'

'I think,' she sighed, 'that I am in a most trying position. I adore Austria and I have many relations there. I am very fond of France and I have some good friends in England. I am torn every way. After all, though,' she went on reflectively, 'it cannot be as hard for me as for you. You really are German, are you not, and yet you have to sit still and see America doing an enormous lot to help the Allies.'

He glanced at her keenly. Her sincerity was undoubted. Before he replied he looked also at the occupants of the next two tables, young people from the land of musical comedy with their khaki-clad escorts, intellectually negligible. Nevertheless, he lowered his voice a little as he answered.

'You are quite right, Miss de Freyne. It is one of the hardest nuts we have to crack, we German-Americans. We are honest and above-board about it, you see. We have worked like slaves to direct the policy of America our own way, and we've failed.'

'Is there nothing more you can do?' she asked earnestly.

There was a moment's silence. Mr. Kessner, with his napkin tucked in underneath his chin, was settling down to his luncheon like a man. Nevertheless, he again glanced searchingly at his neighbour.

'It is hard to see what can be done,' he said calmly. 'I have been in Germany to visit some of my relatives. It is very wonderful to hear them all talk there. There is no pessimism, no doubt whatever, no shadow of misgiving. Germany must win—that is in their hearts. They have not a single doubt. And here in London, whether the people deceive themselves or not, they say the same thing. They go about their business with even more assurance, and they indulge in pleasures far more freely.'

'Which is going to win?' she asked.

'Neither,' he replied. 'Neither has the preponderance of strength to smash the other. It will be a drawn fight. There will be a period of peace, nominal peace. Germany knows now what she has to face—a world in arms against her. When the next time comes, she will be ready.'

'There will be a next time, then?'

'Germany is not yet at the end of her resources,' he assured her. 'There are other ways in which she can make herself felt. But let us leave for a little time these serious subjects. This champagne, I know, my friend Lavendale, is a compliment to me. You English-Americans do not drink champagne in the middle of the day. Believe me, you are wrong. I drink your very good health, Miss de Freyne, and yours, Lavendale. And I drink also,' he added, his eyes lightening a little as he looked across the room, 'the unspoken toast!'

He set his glass down empty.

'There is an unspoken toast close to the heart of all of us, Miss de Freyne,' he remarked, 'one little secret we keep at the back of our thoughts. Now tell me. I sail on Saturday. On Friday night you and our friend Lavendale will give me the honour of your company at dinner, eh? It is arranged. At the Ritz at eight o'clock.'

'You are very kind,' they both murmured

He selected a cigar from a box which had been passed him, and rose a little abruptly.

'I go to speak with a friend,' he said—'a matter of business. For your excellent luncheon I thank you very much, and for the privilege of having met Miss de Freyne,' he added with a little bow, 'I thank you even more. Till Friday, then.'

He shuffled across the room, an ill-dressed, undignified figure, yet with a confidence which surpassed conceit. They saw him greet a compatriot and seat himself at the latter's table.

'That man,' Lavendale said, as he toyed with his coffee spoon, 'has at the back of his head some new scheme. It may not be directed against your people. I have an idea that it is more likely to be directed against mine.'

'But he is an American himself,' she protested.

'He is a German-American,' Lavendale replied, 'which means that he is very much a German and very little an American.'

'Whatever his new scheme may be,' she sighed, 'I do not think that he is disposed to talk about it.'

'Whatever it may be,' Lavendale replied, 'it is my business to find it out. One thing is absolutely certain. No American would receive the attentions of the Kaiser—in war time, too—and come back here without a word to say about it, unless there was something in the background, something he meant to keep secret.'

They strolled out into the entrance hall and Lavendale departed in search of his hat. A waiter came hurriedly out to Suzanne's side.

'For madame,' he whispered, slipping a little note into her hand.

Her fingers closed upon it quickly. She glanced around. Lavendale was still talking to some acquaintances. She opened it and read the few hastily pencilled lines:—

'It would give me a great deal of pleasure to see you again before Friday. I am in flat 74 in the Court here. Shall be alone all this afternoon.'

She crumpled up the note in her hand. Lavendale was coming towards her.

'Can I take you anywhere?' he asked. 'The car will be outside.'

She shook her head.

'Don't bother about me,' she said. 'I am going up to my room to write some letters.'

*****

'Come in!'

Suzanne turned the handle of number seventy-four, closed the door behind her and entered the sitting-room. Mr. Kessner turned around in his chair from before a mass of papers. He looked at Suzanne for an instant in surprise, an expression which, as he recognized her, changed quickly into one of satisfaction. He rose to his feet and came towards her.

'This is a great pleasure, my dear young lady,' he said. 'I scarcely dared to hope——'

He took her hands, but she evaded him with a little smile.

'You see, we are neighbours almost,' she explained. 'I have an apartment here when I am in London. I thought I would call in and see you on the way to my room. But, please—do you mind?'

She pushed him gently away from her. For a moment his face darkened. Then, with a shrug of the shoulders, he threw himself into the easy-chair opposite, a shapeless, ill-dressed little morsel of humanity, with a queer intelligence shining out of his narrowed eyes, suggested, too, in the square forehead and puckered brows.

'Listen, young lady,' he said. 'Do you know why I asked you to come and see me?'

She raised her eyebrows and laughed at him.

'Because you like me, I hope,' she replied. 'For myself, I love making fresh acquaintances amongst clever men.'

'Acquaintances?' he repeated slowly.

She nodded several times.

'I am not one of those,' she said, 'who can gather the whole world in without a pause. I like to make acquaintances. Sometimes an acquaintance may become a friend. Sometimes—but that takes time.'

She felt the steely light of his eyes upon her and looked modestly down upon the carpet.

'Well,' he went on, 'there were two reasons why I sent for you. One I think you have surmised, and you keep it there at the back of your pretty little head. The other—well, you are a young person of intelligence and mixed nationality. I thought it possible that you might be of use to me.'

'But in what manner?' she demanded.

'I was frank with you at luncheon-time,' he said. 'You know where my sympathies lie. Yours, I gathered, are divided. Would it be possible, I wonder, to induce you to look my way?'

'But you yourself admitted,' she reminded him, 'that the cause of Germany in America is lost. What more is there to be done?'

'Young lady,' he replied, 'the cause of Germany in America may be lost for the moment so far as regards our efforts to induce the present administration to carry into effect an ethical neutrality. But the great source of Germany's greatness is her capacity for looking ahead. If one cause is lost, then in that day a new one is born. If Germany had not foreseen and prepared for this war for forty years, she would have been crushed to-day. Now we who are her sons in foreign countries, our eyes, too, are fixed upon the future.'

'Then you have a new scheme,' she said quietly.

'We have a new scheme,' he admitted, 'but what that may be it is not my intention to tell you at present.'

She pouted at once.

'Of course, if you are not going to trust me——'

'You must not be a foolish child,' he interrupted. 'You would think little of me if I did, and besides,' he added, rising to his feet, 'I am not sure yet that I do trust you. Wait.'

He touched the bell. Almost immediately the door of the sitting-room was opened. She gave a little start. An immense coloured man in dark clothes stood respectfully in the doorway.

'George,' his master directed, 'if any one rings, I am engaged. See that I am not disturbed on any pretext.'

'Very good, Mr. Kessner!

The man closed the door with wonderful softness. Even his footsteps, as he retreated into the bedroom, were inaudible. Kessner's elbow was propped against the mantelpiece, his head supported in his thin, yellow-stained fingers. He looked down at her.

'If you do not trust me,' she persisted, 'how can I be of help to you?'

'I might put you to the test,' he said slowly.

There was nothing distinctly threatening in his tone, and yet all at once she was afraid. The thought of that black Hercules loitering outside, something in the downward droop of the eyes of this man all the time edging a little nearer to her, seemed suddenly to become terrifying. Nevertheless, she refused to flinch.

'I do not like riddles,' she declared. 'Perhaps you had better think over more definitely what you want to say to me, before Friday night, or send a note up to my room.'

'There is no necessity,' he replied. 'What I have to say to you is already quite clear in my mind.'

He moved still nearer, stood over the couch by her side. Then the outside bell rang. He paused to listen. Her heart gave a little jump as a familiar voice asked for Mr. Kessner.

'It is Mr. Lavendale!' she exclaimed under her breath. 'Don't let him find me here!'

His features relaxed. He laughed and patted her hand. She could have said nothing to inspire him with more confidence.

'Of course not,' he replied indulgently. 'Don't be afraid. George would tell him that I was engaged. He had my orders to let no one in.'

'But I heard him say that he would wait!' she persisted anxiously. 'Cannot I hide somewhere for a moment while you see him and send him away?'

George made a discreet appearance.

'A gentleman inquiring for you, sir,' he said. 'He is waiting outside in the corridor. I told him that you would be a long time.'

Mr. Kessner considered for a moment.

'Would you mind stepping into my sleeping apartment?' he asked Suzanne.

She sprang up at once.

'You will get rid of him quickly?' she begged.

He pressed her hand affectionately. She endured his touch without flinching. He handed her over to George and pointed to the door of his room.

'Give the young lady a chair inside,' he ordered. 'I will see Mr. Lavendale.'

She was ushered into a bedroom and a moment or two later she heard Lavendale announced. Then George returned, handed her some American papers and disappeared into the bathroom beyond. She rose to her feet as he closed the door. The sound of Lavendale's voice was muffled and inaudible. She glanced around the room. It was tastefully but very plainly furnished. There was nothing about on the mantelpiece or bureau likely to be of the slightest interest. Suddenly her heart gave a little jump. George came out of the bathroom with a coat upon his arm, threw open the bureau and searched there for something. As he stood there, a thin, black silk pocket-book slipped from the breast-pocket of the coat and fell unnoticed on to the carpet. A moment later he closed the bureau, laid the coat carefully out upon the bed and withdrew into the bathroom, closing the door. Suzanne held her breath for a single moment. Then she stole across the floor, seized the pocket-book, opened the bedroom door stealthily, and with a little gulp of relief passed out into the corridor. She ran up the stairs to her own room, gripping the pocket-book in her hand. Arrived there, she locked the door, took up the telephone and spoke to the hall-porter.

'Please don't let Mr. Lavendale go out,' she directed. 'When he comes downstairs send him up to my room—say that I wish to see him at once.'

She slipped the pocket-book into the bosom of her dress and waited. In a few minutes there was a ring at the bell. Lavendale stood outside.

'Come in at once,' she begged.

He hesitated, but she dragged him in.

'Do not be foolish!' she exclaimed. 'Shut the door. You have just left Mr. Kessner?'

'Yes,' he admitted.

'Why did you go there?'

'To see if you were getting yourself into any trouble,' he answered grimly.

'You knew?'

He nodded.

'Yes, I knew!'

She drew the pocket-book from the bosom of her gown.

'Listen,' she said, 'I am terrified. I picked this up from the bedroom. It slipped out of the pocket of his dinner-coat. I haven't even dared to look inside.'

He moved to the door and locked it, came back and shook the contents out on to the table. There was a great roll of notes, some visiting cards, some notes copied from a German time-table, a long list of names, and a single letter on thick, cream paper. Suzanne stole to the door on tiptoe and stood there, listening. There was no sound in the corridor, no sound in the apartment at all except a smothered exclamation or two from Lavendale. Presently he called to her. He was holding the papers in his hand.

'Miss de Freyne,' he whispered, 'listen.'

She caught him by the sleeve. There was a ponderous knocking at the door, the shrill summons of the bell rang through the room. Lavendale hesitated for a moment. Then he slipped the book into his inside pocket and threw open the door. Mr. Kessner's black servant was standing outside.

'The master has sent his compliments,' he said, 'and would be glad to know——'

He glanced at Suzanne. It was obvious that Lavendale's presence in the room embarrassed him. Then he was suddenly pushed on one side and back into the corridor. Mr. Kessner himself came quietly in and closed the door behind him. There was a queer little gleam in his eyes, but his manner was unruffled. He tried the handle of the door to be sure that it was closed. Then he turned towards Suzanne.

'Will a million dollars,' he asked, 'buy me back my pocket-book?'

Lavendale drew it from his pocket and promptly handed it across.

'My dear Mr. Kessner,' he remonstrated, 'you are surely not serious! Miss de Freyne was just explaining her little escapade to me and I was coming in search of you.'

Mr. Kessner took no notice of either of them for several moments. He ran through the contents of the pocket-book, then he slowly thrust it into his pocket.

'I shall have the pleasure,' he said, 'on Friday night? You will not forget—the Ritz at eight o'clock?'

'Charmed,' Lavendale murmured.

'Delighted,' Suzanne faltered.

He made a little bow—an ugly, awkward bow—and left the room. There was nothing in his manner to indicate what his sensations were. Lavendale and Suzanne looked at one another.

'Was there anything very important there?' she asked.

He laughed.

'Nothing from your point of view, but everything from mine,' he told her. 'There was a list of forty-two names of German-Americans, each giving a million dollars towards a specific purpose. There was a plan of a few remaining estates in a certain part of Brazil, still to be purchased to establish what at some seasonable juncture should be declared to be a German colony. Some slight trouble with the Government of Brazil, a German gunboat, and behold!—German South America and to Hell with the Monroe Doctrine! A very admirable scheme, only——'

'Only what?'

'I don't fancy that, thanks to you, those estates will ever come into the market,' he remarked dryly, 'not for a German purchaser, at any rate.'

She glanced uneasily towards the door.

'Mr. Lavendale,' she said earnestly 'I am terrified!'

'Why?'

'I am afraid of Mr. Kessner,' she confessed. 'He took it much too quietly.'

Lavendale shrugged his shoulders.

'A man of his temperament,' he said, 'seldom wastes his time or his emotions. He was playing for a great stake which he knows now that he will lose. At the same time, he has lost purely through accident.'

She suddenly smiled.

'I wonder,' she exclaimed, 'whether he really expects us to dine with him at the Ritz on Friday night!'

'We'll go and see, at any rate,' Lavendale declared.

CHAPTER VI.
THE MACHINATIONS OF MR. COURLANDER

Lavendale glanced at his thin gold watch and replaced it in his waistcoat pocket.

'Three minutes past eight,' he remarked. 'Half a dozen pairs of gloves for me, I think. Shall I go in and see about a table or would you rather dine somewhere else?'

Suzanne made a little grimace. They were in the foyer of the Ritz Hotel, and she was wearing a wonderful new gown.

'It is most disappointing,' she declared. 'I had made up my mind to conquest.'

'I am very impressionable,' Lavendale assured her.

She shook her head petulantly.

'It is not you whom I wish to subjugate.'

'I am too easy a victim, I suppose,' Lavendale sighed. 'I am afraid that to-night, however, you will have to be content with me.'

Her face suddenly changed, a brilliant smile parted her lips, she glanced at him triumphantly. Lavendale looked over his shoulder. Mr. Kessner was crossing the lounge towards them with outstretched hand.

'You've lost your gloves,' Suzanne murmured under her breath.

Mr. Kessner greeted his two guests in the most matter-of-fact fashion.

'I must apologize for being a few moments late,' he said. 'It is rather crowded here to-night, and I thought it best to go and see that no mistake had been made about my table. I should like, if I may, to introduce to you Mr. Courlander, a friend of mine from New York. Mr. Courlander is dining with us.'

The two young people murmured something suitable. Mr. Courlander turned out to be a dark, heavy-browed man, clean-shaven, and of a taciturn disposition. The little party made their way in to dinner. They were ushered to a small round table in the best quarter of the room, a table lavishly arranged with flowers and flanked with a couple of ice-pails, from which gold-foiled bottles were protruding. Suzanne gave a little sigh of content as she sank into her chair, and looked around her appreciatively.

'I have always observed,' she said softly, 'that the men of your country, Mr. Kessner, know so well how to entertain.'

'And also,' Mr. Kessner remarked, blinking slightly, 'how to select their guests.'

The service of dinner proceeded. Mr. Kessner, in his dress-suit, which seemed several sizes too large for him, appeared somehow to have become a more insignificant person than ever. In this ultra-fashionable restaurant, full of well-set-up men and soldiers in uniform, he seemed almost like some by-product, something not altogether human. His very insignificance compelled a certain amount of notice; conferred upon him, perhaps, an air of distinctiveness if not of distinction. He was Kessner, the multi-millionaire, probably over to secure contracts from the Government. The aroma of wealth hovered around his table. The term 'German-American' was unused—to few people there did it convey any significance. The little party talked of every subject under the sun except the war. Mr. Courlander, notwithstanding his heavy appearance, was an excellent raconteur. Dinner was more than half-way through before their host changed his attitude.

'You two young people did not, by any chance, expect me to break my appointment for this evening, did you?' he asked.

'We had a bet about it,' Suzanne admitted.

'Tell me who wagered in my favour and I will tell you which is the cleverer of the two?' he offered.

Suzanne laughed.

'It was I who thought that you would come,' she declared.

He bowed.

'After all,' he argued, 'why not? Listen,' he went on, leaning across the table. 'Courlander here does not count. He is in my confidence. He was, indeed, at one time my private secretary. To the world I am an American. To our young friend here,' he went on, indicating Lavendale, 'who appears to have partly discarded his diplomatic career for an excursion into the secret service of his country, I am a German-American. He follows me to Germany. He knows that I have a conference with the Kaiser. He is all agog with the importance of it. He comes back. He consults with you, my dear young lady, and with marvellous subtlety he asks me to lunch and exposes me most unfairly to the trial of your charms. I succumb—what more natural?'

He leaned back in his chair while a portly *maîtres d'hôtel* superintended the filling of their glasses with champagne and explained to him the mysteries of the course which was being served. Neither Suzanne nor Lavendale found it easy to continue their meal unmoved. Their eyes were fixed upon this insignificant little man who spoke with such deliberation, such a queer little curl of the lips, such obvious enjoyment of his own thoughts.

'Your deep-laid scheme,' he went on, 'was crowned with complete success. The poor little American was robbed of his secret. By this time it is probably known in Washington. There is only one little fly in the ointment. A private intimation has already been given through our ambassador in Washington to the American Government, that unless America at once abandons her position of favouring the Allies at the expense of Germany and Austria, Germany will refuse now and for always henceforth to respect and accept the Monroe Doctrine.'

There was a moment's breathless silence. Then Lavendale drained his glass.

'You mean that that pronouncement has already been made?' he murmured.

'It has already been made,' Mr. Kessner assented. 'Further, you can understand quite easily, I am sure, that the exact locality in which this break should take place, although interesting, is not of vital importance. I do not wish to dispirit you. Yours was, without doubt, an excellent stroke of work, and I, the poor victim, am compelled to droop a diminished head. Yet I offer you this explanation so that you can see the reason why I am able to accept my defeat gracefully, to welcome you both here as my guests, to raise my glass to your beautiful eyes, mademoiselle, and to wish you, Mr. Lavendale, the further success in your profession which such subtlety and finesse demand.'

'Say, he's eloquent to-night, isn't he?' Mr. Courlander remarked. 'Quite an epic little meeting, this. I can assure you all that I consider it an immense privilege to have been asked to join your little party this evening.'

'My subtle friend,' Mr. Kessner continued, setting his glass down empty, 'is now wondering why you were asked to join it.'

'Not at all,' Lavendale replied. 'The fame of Mr. Courlander is well known to me.'

Their host for a single moment seemed disturbed. He recovered himself, however, almost immediately.

'Mr. Courlander,' he went on, 'as I have told you was once my secretary. Since then, for a brief space of time, he became a criminologist. Disgusted with the coarse tendencies of crime as practised in more modern cities he abandoned that profession to become what I might call a diplomatic detective. He is the terror of our loose-living public men and our ambitious but dishonest politicians.'

'Our friend's career in America,' Lavendale remarked dryly, 'must of necessity be a strenuous one!'

Mr. Kessner for a moment smiled. There was no effort of humour about the gesture. It was simply a slow, sideways parting of the lips, an index of thoughts travelling backwards along a road lined with grotesque memories. He drew a heavy gold pencil from his pocket and signed the bill. Then he rose to his feet.

'We will take our coffee outside,' he suggested. 'Afterwards, if it meets with your approval, I have a box at one of the music halls—I am not sure which.'

They lingered only a few minutes over their coffee. While they sat there, however, Mr. Kessner's secretary, a middle-aged man with gold spectacles and abstracted manner, brought in a note. Mr. Kessner opened it, read it carefully and tore it into small pieces. He rose, a few minutes later, joined his secretary, who was waiting on the outskirts of the little group, and walked with him twice down the entrance hall. Then he returned.

'The car is waiting,' he announced, 'if you are ready. Won't you, my Machiavellian young friend,' he added, glancing at the scraps of paper which he had left upon the coffee table, 'try and put those fragments together? I promise that you would find them interesting—more intrigue, and a very interesting one, I can assure you.'

Lavendale found it hard to forgive himself later for the impulse which prompted his answer. The temptation, however, was irresistible.

'I have no need to put them together to know the source of your message,' he replied.

'No?' Mr. Kessner remarked politely, as he lingered for a moment over adjusting Suzanne's coat. 'There are a good many millions of people in London, are there not? Shall I give you a hundred thousand to one against naming the writer?'

'In dollars, if you like,' Lavendale replied carelessly. 'I won't take your money, but I'll start, then, with Baron Niko Komashi.'

Mr. Kessner, who had half turned away, watching the result of his attentions to Suzanne, became suddenly motionless. His lips were a little parted, he seemed almost paralysed. When he turned slowly around there was a new look in his eyes. Courlander, on the other hand, did not attempt to restrain an exclamation of wonder.

'Baron Niko Komashi,' Kessner repeated. 'Who is he?'

Lavendale laughed easily. He was already bitterly regretting his momentary lapse.

'Heaven knows!' he exclaimed. 'The odds dazzled me.'

They walked out to the car almost in silence. A new spirit seemed to have come to Kessner. He looked and talked differently throughout the rest of the evening's entertainment. He seemed somehow to have lost his air of half bantering confidence. When the time came for farewells, he looked long and earnestly into Lavendale's face.

'We must know one another better, young man,' was all he said....

On their way back to her rooms, Suzanne gripped Lavendale by the arm and asked him a question.

'What does it all mean?' she demanded. 'Why did you guess Niko? Why were they both so thunderstruck?'

'Because,' he replied, 'Niko happened to be the writer of that little epistle.'

Her large eyes gleamed at him through the semi-darkness, filled with wonder.

'But how could you possibly know that?'

He smiled.

'It is your responsibility,' he explained. 'I noticed the perfume directly he drew the note from the envelope.'

She laughed softly—softly at first and then heartily.

'Why, it is most amusing!' she exclaimed. 'He thinks you a necromancer. He is, I believe, a little afraid of you. And that other man, all through the performance he scarcely took his eyes off you.'

'At any rate,' Lavendale observed, 'it has given me something to think about.'

II

Lavendale found his way to the American Embassy early on the following morning, and interviewed his friend Mr. Washburn.

'Anything from Washington?' he inquired.

'I have only had a formal acknowledgment,' Mr. Washburn replied, 'except that they added a code word they don't often make use of, and which I take to indicate a pat on the back for you.'

'Is it true,' Lavendale continued, dragging a chair up to the side of Mr. Washburn's desk, 'that Berlin has given Washington to understand that unless she changes her attitude toward the Allies and withdraws her objection to submarine warfare, she will no longer respect the Monroe Doctrine?'

'*Pourparlers* to that effect,' Mr. Washburn confessed, 'have passed. How did you come to hear of them?'

Lavendale smiled a little grimly, yet with some self-satisfaction.

'I am getting on the track of something else which promises to be even more interesting,' he went on. 'Tell me, how do we stand with Japan just now?'

Mr. Washburn knitted his brows.

'Still friction—always friction,' he admitted. 'The whole thing is too ridiculous. Personally, I consider our Western States are very much to blame. We have never before raised the cry 'America for the Americans only,' and it's too late to do it now. And the fact of it is you see, the Western States simply decline to fall in with Washington Policy. Then the trouble comes. Any particular reason for asking?'

'I don't know yet,' Lavendale replied. 'There's a Japanese fellow named Komashi in my line of business, seems to be very busy just lately. I only caught on to it last night, though. Chief well?'

'We are all overworked,' Washburn replied. 'We have had to send Barclay over to Berlin to get a personal report about the prisoners' camps there. Then we get enough questions from Germany ourselves, about their prisoners here, to swamp the place.'

Lavendale took up his hat.

'I'll see you later,' he promised.

He walked down the steps from Spring Gardens into St. James's Park and sat for a time upon a seat. Exactly in front of him, the upper floors of one of the big houses in Carlton Terrace had been turned into a hospital, and he could see the soldiers lying about in long chairs, a few of them entertaining guests. Behind him was the long row of huts built by the Admiralty. A troop of soldiers swung along the broad road, a loudly playing band heralded the approach of a little company of recruits. Save for these things, London seemed as usual. From where he sat, the hum and the roar of the great city came as insistently as ever to his ears. His thoughts had travelled back to New York. How long, he wondered? ...

It was one of the chances of a lifetime which brought Lavendale face to face that afternoon with Baron Niko Komashi in a quiet street near St. James's Square. Niko would have passed on without even a sign of recognition but Lavendale stopped him.

'Good afternoon!' he said.

'Good afternoon!' the other replied gravely.

'I should like a few minutes' conversation with you,' Lavendale proceeded.

Niko was perplexed but acquiescent.

'If it pleases,' he answered a little vaguely.

Lavendale marched him along the street.

'There is a little bridge club to which I belong, close at hand,' he said. 'Come into the sitting-room there for a few moments. We shall be quite alone at this hour of the afternoon.'

Niko suffered himself to be passively led in the direction which his companion indicated. In a few moments they were seated in the comfortable parlour of a well-known bridge club. They were quite alone and Lavendale closed the door.

'Well,' he asked, 'how goes it with your new ally?'

Niko's face betrayed nothing but mild wonder. Lavendale smiled.

'Listen,' he said, 'I may be making a mistake about you. I do not think that I am. I think that you represent for your country what I do for mine. You are intensely patriotic. So am I. You realize the need for a certain amount of diplomatic insight into the workings of her constitution and her future. So do I. The only trouble is that you are for Japan and I am for America.'

Niko assented very gravely. His soft brown eyes were watching Lavendale's lips as though they would read upon them even the unuttered words. His finger-tips, soft and pliant as velvet, were pressed together.

'You are not to be bought, my friend,' Lavendale went on. 'Neither am I. When we walk together, you hedge yourself around with restraint because you believe that I am one of those who could bear your country ill-will. That is where you are wrong. That is where there is a cloud between us which ought to be driven away. Japan and America naturally, industrially and geographically, should be friends, not enemies.'

'The causes of ill-feeling which lie between us,' Niko observed suavely, 'are not of our making.'

'Nor of ours—not of the true American,' Lavendale answered promptly. 'It is the desire of Washington, official Washington, that the sons of your country who come to us should be treated as our own sons. What we have to contend with, and you, is local feeling. The only sentiment that exists against Japan in my country is that local feeling, and the people who have shown themselves most virulently possessed of it are the compatriots of the man who only within the last few weeks has sought to pave the way for a disgraceful compact with your country.'

Niko's face was a little whiter, his eyes were filled with wonder. Slowly he nodded his head.

'You surprise me with your knowledge of things which I had imagined secret,' he said. 'Secret they have remained so far as I am concerned. Such information as you have gained can have come but from one source, so I will speak thus far. The sword of Japan shall be drawn in defence of her honour, and for no other cause. The alliance which you suggest would be hateful and dishonouring to my country. Nor,' he concluded, 'would Japan at any time commence a war with a treasonable ally.'

'What answer have you made to Kessner?' Lavendale asked bluntly.

His companion gently raised his eyebrows.

'Who is that gentleman—Mr. Kessner?' he inquired.

Lavendale shrugged his shoulders.

'Ah! I forgot,' he said. 'Those would not be your methods. Yet we know quite well that the person whose name I have mentioned has made overtures to you which could not, under present circumstances, emanate from Berlin. Japan from the west, and Germany on the east, might well embarrass a country so criminally unprepared for war as mine. I take it, however, that that combination is not to be feared.'

Niko rose from his place. He had a habit of ending a discussion exactly at the period he chose.

'Not in your time or mine,' he answered simply....

Lavendale, notwithstanding a nervous system almost unexampled, was possessed of curiously sensitive instincts. Before he reached Pall Mall, he was obsessed with an idea that he was being followed. He turned rather abruptly around. A tall, broad-shouldered man in dark clothes, wearing a Homburg hat and with a cigar in the corner of his mouth, waved his stick in friendly greeting.

'This is Mr. Lavendale, isn't it?' he remarked. 'Kind of forgotten me, perhaps? My name's Courlander. Met you with Mr. Kessner the other night.'

'I remember you perfectly,' Lavendale acknowledged. 'Very pleasant dinner we had.'

Mr. Courlander fell into step with his companion, who had turned eastwards.

'There are few things in the world that Ludwig Kessner doesn't understand,' he continued, 'from the placing of a loan to the ordering of a dinner. He isn't much use at eating it, poor fellow, but that's the fault of his digestion. Too much ice-water, I tell him.'

Lavendale nodded affably. He had no objection whatever to discussing Mr. Kessner.

'Kind of misunderstood over here, the boss,' Courlander went on. 'People think because he's of German extraction that his sympathies are altogether that way. As a matter of fact, I can tell you, Mr. Lavendale, that people are dead wrong. At the present moment—I wouldn't have every one know this, but you're an American, too—Mr. Kessner is making proposals for a very large purchase of British War Loan.'

'Is he indeed!' Lavendale observed, in a tone as colourless as he could make it.

Courlander glanced at him curiously. They were passing the Carlton and he drew his arm through Lavendale's.

'Just one cocktail,' he suggested.

Lavendale hesitated for a moment, inspired by an instinctive dislike of his companion. Policy, however, intervened. He accepted the invitation and followed Courlander into the smoke-room. They found two easy-chairs and the latter gave the order.

'I was talking about the boss,' he went on. 'There are others besides you who have misunderstood him some, but they'll learn the truth before the war's over.'

'When is Mr. Kessner returning to America?' Lavendale asked.

'As soon as he can find a safe steamer,' Courlander replied. 'He is a trifle nervous about the Atlantic. Say, that tastes good!'

Mr. Courlander leaned back and sipped his cocktail. Lavendale, with a word of excuse, rose to his feet and strolled across the room to speak to an acquaintance. He returned in less than a minute. Mr. Courlander was leaning back in his chair, American from tip to toe. He wore a dark grey suit of some smooth material. His square-toed boots, the little flag in his buttonhole, his prim tie, his air of genial confidence, were all eloquently and convincingly typical of his nationality. Lavendale was followed by a waiter bearing two more glasses upon a tray.

'Try my sort,' he invited.

Mr. Courlander glanced at Lavendale's glass, which was still three-quarters full.

'You haven't finished your first one yet,' he remarked.

'A little too dry for me,' Lavendale replied, placing it upon the tray and taking the full glass. 'Here's luck!'

The two men looked at one another. In Courlander's hard brown eyes, a little narrowed by his drooping eyebrows, there was an air of fierce though latent questioning. Then with an abrupt gesture he took the glass from the tray and drank off its contents.

'You'll forgive me if I hurry away,' Lavendale went on. 'We shall meet again, I dare say, before Mr. Kessner leaves.'

'Sure!' Mr. Courlander murmured, as he picked up his hat. 'I am generally to be found round about the Milan. Like to have you come and dine with me one night.'

The two men parted at the hotel entrance. Lavendale got into a taxi and drove to his rooms. As he changed his clothes, he glanced through his correspondence. There was a note from Suzanne which he read over twice: —

'Dear Friend, –

'I want to see you at once. I shall be in
from seven till eight. Please call.'

Lavendale glanced at the clock, hurried with his toilet, and found himself ringing the bell at the entrance door of Suzanne's suite at half-past seven. She admitted him herself and ushered him into the little sitting-room, which had been transformed almost into a bower of deep red roses.

'Mr. Kessner,' she exclaimed, pointing around, 'with a carte de visite! You see what he says? —'"From a forgiving enemy!"'

Lavendale glanced at them with a frown upon his forehead.

'I'd like to throw them out of the window,' he declared frankly.

'Do not be foolish,' she laughed. 'Listen. You are dining somewhere?'

'At our own shop,' he replied. 'They ask me about once in every two months, to fill up.'

'I wanted to speak to you about that man Courlander,' she went on.

'Well?'

'Lawrence Dowell—the American newspapers woman, you know—was in here yesterday and stayed to lunch. We saw Mr. Courlander in the distance and she told me about him. Do you know that he was convicted of murder?—that it was only through Mr. Kessner's influence that he was taken out of Sing-Sing? He was a police-sergeant and his name was Drayton. They say that there were several cases against him of having men put out of the way who had made themselves obnoxious to Tammany Hall. The sentence against him was quite clear, yet Mr. Kessner not only managed to have him released but made him his private secretary.'

Lavendale stood for a moment looking out of the window with his hands in his pockets. Then he turned slowly around.

'About an hour ago,' he said, 'this fellow Courlander tried to doctor a cocktail I was drinking in the Carlton smoking-room.'

'What?' she exclaimed.

'I met him at the corner of St. James's Street,' he went on. 'I had been in the club with Niko Komashi, and I am perfectly certain that he had been dogging me. We walked along Pall Mall and he pressed me to go in and have a cocktail. I happened to cross the room to speak to Willoughby and on the way glanced into the mirror. I saw Courlander's hand suddenly flash over my glass. It was so quick that even though I saw it myself, I could scarcely believe it, and I'm certain that no one else in the room could have noticed it. When I got back, I made some excuse and ordered another cocktail.'

She seemed suddenly to lose some part of that serenity which as yet he had never seen even ruffled. She was distinctly paler.

'You must be careful—please promise that you will be careful,' she begged.

'This isn't New York,' he reminded her.

'But that man is a perfect devil,' she persisted earnestly. 'He is a professional murderer. He has no feeling, no mercy, and he is so cunning. And behind him there is Kessner and all his millions.'

Lavendale shrugged his shoulders.

'All the millions that were ever owned,' he said, 'wouldn't help a man over here against the law. I am not afraid of Courlander. There is nothing he could try which I am not prepared for, and if it comes to a hand-to-hand struggle, I don't think I have anything to fear from him.'

'I don't like it,' she told him frankly. 'You will be on your guard, won't you?'

His voice softened.

'Of course I will, but, Miss de Freyne—Suzanne—why don't you like it? Why do you worry about me at all?'

She was silent for a moment. She had turned a little towards the window, her eyes had lost their usual directness. He took a step forward.

'It isn't because you care a little about me, by any chance, is it?' he asked.

She gave him her hand. Then she turned around and he saw that her eyes were soft with tears.

'Suzanne!' he faltered.

She turned towards him. There was something very sweet about her little gesture, something yielding and yet restraining.

'Won't you please forget all this for just a little time?' she pleaded. 'To tell you the truth, I feel almost like a traitress when I even let myself think of such things now that my country is in such agony, when everything that is dear to me in life seems imperilled. You have your work, too, and I have mine. Perhaps the end may be happy.'

He raised her fingers to his lips and kissed them.

'I will obey,' he promised, turning towards the door.

'And you will be careful—please be careful,' she begged, as she let him out and squeezed his arm for a moment. 'There! Now you must go to your dinner. You look very nice, and I am sure you will sit next some one altogether charming, and perhaps you will forget. But I shall like to think of this evening.' ...

Practical, hard-headed, and with a sound hold upon the every-day episodes of life, Lavendale nevertheless passed through the remainder of that evening with his head in the clouds. He was vaguely conscious of the other twenty-three guests who shared with him the hospitality of the Ambassador—a few diplomats, a professor from Harvard University and his wife, two other distinguished

Americans, with a sprinkling of their English connections. He sat next a distant relative of his own, an American girl who had married an Englishman, and his abstraction was perhaps ministered to by the fact that conversation from him was entirely unlooked for. In the reception rooms afterwards he found himself able to speak for a moment with Washburn.

'Have you seen anything of Mr. Kessner?' he asked.

The other made a little grimace.

'Very little,' he replied. 'The Chief and he don't exactly hit it off. I heard a rumour the other day that he might be going back to Germany.'

Lavendale played a couple of rubbers of bridge and was invited to take a cigar in the library before he left. It was shortly after one o'clock before he stepped into the taxicab which a servant had summoned for him.

'17 Sackville Street,' Lavendale directed.

He threw himself back in the corner of the vehicle, and they glided off. A drizzling rain was falling and the streets were almost empty. He leaned forward in his place to light a cigarette. That fact and his habits of observation probably saved his life. He realized suddenly that this was no ordinary taxicab in which he was travelling. It conformed to none of the usual types. The cushions were more luxurious, the appointments unusual. He sat for a moment thinking. The chauffeur was driving at a fair pace, but he had taken a somewhat circuitous route. Lavendale tried the doors, first on one side, then on the other. They were both fast, secured with some sort of spring lock. Suddenly alert, he rose softly to his feet, crouched for a moment upon the back seat and thrust his head and shoulders through the window. It was easy enough to wriggle out, to descend and allow the vehicle to proceed to its destination, wherever that might be, without its passenger, but the love of adventure was upon him. He set his teeth, sank back once more in his corner, half closed his eyes. To all appearance he might have been a tired diner-out prematurely asleep. As a matter of fact, every nerve and sense was keenly on the alert, and his right fingers were locked around the butt of a small revolver. Without protest or comment, he saw himself conducted by a roundabout way into a maze of quiet streets. Then, with a little thrill of anticipation, he saw a man who had been loitering near an entry turn and follow the vehicle, which at his coming had slackened speed. The man was wearing some sort of rubber-soled shoes and his footsteps upon the street were noiseless. Through his half-closed eyes, Lavendale was nevertheless conscious of his approach, realized his soft spring on to the footboard of the car, was more than prepared for the sudden flick in his face of a sodden towel, reeking with chloroform. His right fist shot out, the figure on the footboard went reeling back into the street. Even then, prepared though he had been, Lavendale for a moment gasped for breath. The car, with a sudden grinding of the brakes, came to a standstill. They were at the top of a darkly-lit street and not a soul was in sight. Lavendale thrust his foot through the glass in front of him, shattering it all around the driver. The man half sprang to his feet, but Lavendale's swift speech arrested him.

'Sit where you are,' he ordered. 'Never mind about that other fellow. Drive me to the Milan Hotel. You know the way, so do I. If you go a yard out of it, feel this!'

He suddenly dug the muzzle of his revolver into the man's neck. The man, with an oath, crouched forward.

'Do as I tell you,' Lavendale thundered, 'or I'll shoot you where you sit! Remember you're not in New York. Do as I tell you.'

Once more the car glided off. They turned almost immediately into Piccadilly, across Leicester Square, passed up the Strand and drew up at the Milan. Lavendale put his head through the window as the porter came out from the Court entrance.

'I can't open this door,' he said. 'Ask the fellow in front how to do it.'

The porter stared with surprise at the shattered glass. The driver slipped down, touched a spring on the outside and the door flew open. He had pulled his cap deeper over his face. Lavendale looked at him for a moment steadfastly.

'Wait for me,' he ordered.

He walked into the Court, rang for the lift and ascended to the fourth floor. He stepped out and rang the bell at number seventy-four. For a moment there was no answer. He rang it again. Then a light suddenly flashed up in the room and Mr. Kessner, fully dressed, stood upon the threshold. He gazed, speechless, at Lavendale, who pushed forward across the threshold, holding the door open with one hand.

'Mr. Kessner,' he said, 'your thug with the chloroform is lying on his back somewhere near Sackville Street. I shouldn't wonder if his spine wasn't broken. Your sham chauffeur is downstairs with his sham taxicab. I made him bring me here. You understand?'

The tip of Mr. Kessner's tongue had moistened his lips. His lined yellow face seemed more than ever like the face of some noxious animal.

'You are drunk, young man,' he said.

Lavendale raised his arm and Mr. Kessner stepped back.

'Don't be afraid,' Lavendale went on scornfully. 'I am not going to shoot you. When the day of reckoning comes between you and me, if ever it does, I shall take you by the throat and wring the life out of your body. But I am here now to tell you this. Before I sleep, a full account of this night's adventure, instigated by you and your assassin Courlander, will be written down and deposited in a safe place. If anything happens to me, if I disappear even for a dozen hours, that paper will be opened. You may get me, even now, you and Courlander between you, only you'll have to pay the price. See? In England it's a damned ugly price!'

Mr. Kessner sucked the breath in between his teeth. Then, as though with some super-human effort, he recovered himself.

'Say, young fellow, won't you come in and talk this out?' he invited.

Lavendale laughed dryly.

'"Won't you walk into my parlour?"' he quoted mockingly. 'No, thank you, Mr. Kessner! You know where we stand now. Let me give you a word of warning. London isn't New York. A very little of this sort of thing and you'll find the hand of a law that can't be bought or bribed or evaded in any way, tapping upon your shoulders. You understand?'

Mr. Kessner yawned.

'You are a foolish young man,' he said, 'and you've been reading a little too much modern fiction.'

He slammed the door and Lavendale descended to the street. The courtyard was empty.

'The car didn't wait for me, I suppose?' he inquired of the porter.

'The fellow drove off directly you went upstairs, sir. I shouted after him but he took no notice. Shall I get you a taxi, sir?'

Lavendale fumbled in his pocket, found a cigarette and lit it.

'Thank you,' he replied, 'I think I'll walk.'

CHAPTER VII.
THE INDISCREET TRAVELLER

Lavendale walked slowly down the sunny side of Pall Mall. It was early in August, and for the first time he seemed to notice some reflection in the faces of the passers-by of the burden under which the country was groaning. The usual fashionable little throng about the entrance to the Carlton, was represented by a few sombrely-dressed women and one or two wounded warriors. The glances of the passers-by towards the contents bill of the evening papers had in them a certain furtive eagerness, the fear of evil news triumphing now over the sanguine optimism of earlier days. It was just at that tragical epoch when Russia, to the amazement of the whole world, was being swept back from her frontier cities, when there were murmurs of an investment of Petrograd. Lavendale, in his light grey suit and straw hat, sunburnt, over six feet tall, broad and athletic, seemed somehow a strange figure as he passed along through streets which appeared destitute of a single man under middle-age who was not in khaki. The recruiting sergeant at the corner of Trafalgar Square, where Lavendale paused for a moment to cross the road, caught his eye and smiled insinuatingly.

'Fine figure for a uniform, sir,' he ventured.

'I am an alien,' Lavendale replied, watching a troop of recruits pass by.

'American, sir?'

'That's so,' Lavendale admitted.

The sergeant looked him up and down and sighed.

'America's a country, begging your pardon, sir, that don't seem to have much stomach for fighting,' he remarked, as the young man passed on.

Lavendale crossed the street with a slight frown upon his forehead. He made his way to the War Office and found Captain Merrill in his room alone. The two men exchanged the greetings of intimate friends.

'Say, Reggie,' Lavendale began, 'you folks are getting kind of nervy, aren't you? A recruiting sergeant in Trafalgar Square has just gently intimated to me that I belong to a country which has no stomach for fighting.'

Merrill grinned as he tossed his cigarette case over.

'Well,' he remarked, 'you don't seem to be exactly spoiling for the fray, do you?'

Lavendale lit a cigarette.

'Look here,' he said, 'it's all very well for you fellows to talk. You've got the war fever in your blood. You're in it deep yourselves and there's a sort of gloomy satisfaction in seeing every one else in the same box. The chap who goes out to provoke a fight is worse, of course, but the one who springs up and reaches for his gun at the first chance of joining in, is playing his game, isn't he?'

'Perhaps you are right,' Merrill admitted.

'I'm not telling you or any one else exactly what my opinion is about America's policy,' Lavendale continued. 'I'll only remind you that, even when those truculent forefathers of ours went out to fight, they stopped to put on their armour. Is there anything fresh?'

'I don't know,' was the somewhat doubtful reply. 'There is a queer sort of feeling of apprehension everywhere this morning. The Chief's been round to see the Prime Minister and on to the Admiralty. There's a rumour that he went round to Buckingham Palace, too. Looks as though there were something up.'

'You know all about it, I suppose,' Lavendale remarked quietly.

'Not a thing!'

The young American knocked the ash from his cigarette.

'The history of this war,' he went on, 'will make mighty interesting reading, but there's another history, a history that will never be written, the history of the unrecorded things. Gee, that would make people gossip if they could get hold of only a few chapters of it! You know there's something strange afoot, Reggie. So do I, though we sit here lying to one another. I doubt whether the man in the street will ever know.'

Merrill selected another cigarette.

'I don't see where you come in here, Ambrose.'

'Neither do I,' the other agreed. 'Still, the truth comes to light in strange ways sometimes. Last night I had a cable from a friend in Petrograd, advising me to buy all Russian securities.'

'Well?'

'If there is to be any change for the better in the valuations of Russian stock,' Lavendale continued slowly, 'that is to say any immediate change, it can only mean one thing.'

Merrill struggled hard to preserve his expression of polite vacuity.

'There are very few people,' he murmured, 'who really understand Russia.'

Lavendale shrugged his shoulders.

'It isn't exactly my show, you know!'

'It ought to be,' Merrill retorted curtly.

'Why?'

'Just common-sense. If we don't win in this war, it will be your turn next. Japan and Germany you'll have to face—you can take my word for that—and I hope you'll like it. If we lose our Fleet, it's good-bye to American independence.'

'Plain and simple words, young fellow!'

'Not so plain or so simple as they are true.'

Lavendale threw away his cigarette and stretched out his hand for his hat.

'Well,' he said, 'I used to flatter myself that I was an out-and-out neutral, but I'm beginning to fancy that my sympathies are leaning a little towards your side of the show. Anyhow, I've no reason to keep secret the little I know about this affair—in fact I came down here to tell you. New York was talking openly last night of peace being proclaimed between Germany and Russia within a week.'

'We've tried her sorely,' Merrill confessed doggedly, 'but I don't believe it.'

Lavendale rose to his feet.

'I tell you, Merrill,' he said, 'if you'd been about town as much as I have for the last twenty-four hours, you'd begin to wonder yourself whether something wasn't amiss. These rumours and feelings of depression are one of the strangest features of the war, but there it is at the present moment, in the streets and the clubs and the restaurants— wherever you turn. I've noticed nothing like it since the beginning of the war. The optimists are still cackling away, but it's there all the same—a grim, disheartening fear. One man told me last night that he knew for a fact that Russia was on the point of suing for peace.'

Merrill shook his head as he resumed his place at his desk.

'It's just a phase,' he declared. 'Look in and see me again, Ambrose, when you're feeling a little more cheerful.' ...

Lavendale made a call in the Strand and passed along that crowded, illuminative thoroughfare towards the Milan. Everywhere the faces of the passers-by seemed indicative of some new apprehension. He bought an early paper, but there was no word in it of any change in the situation. On any printed presentation of the rumours which were on every one's tongue, the censor had set his foot.

Lavendale called in at the bar at the Milan for a few minutes. The same feeling was there even more in evidence.

'What's it all mean?' he asked an American pressman whom he knew slightly.

The newspaper man nodded sagely.

'Guess the cat's out of the bag now,' he opined. 'Russia has asked for peace and she is going to have it on generous terms. They say that negotiations are going on right here, under the Britisher's very nose. Things'll be pretty lively here soon.'

Lavendale took his place in the luncheon-room, a few minutes later. As usual he glanced expectantly towards the corner which Suzanne de Freyne frequently occupied. There were no signs of her to-day, however. He gave his order and leaned back in his place. Then some fancy impelled him to glance towards the glass entrance doors on his left. He sprang at once to his feet. Suzanne, her face whiter than ever, a queer, furtive gleam in her dark eyes, was looking eagerly into the room. She saw him almost at the same moment and hurried in.

'Suzanne!' he exclaimed. 'What luck! You are going to lunch with me, of course?'

A *maître d'hôtel* was holding the vacant chair at his table. With a little sigh she relapsed into it. She was plainly dressed and had the appearance of having newly arrived from a journey.

'I suppose I had better have something to eat,' she sighed. 'Order something—anything,' she added, brushing the carte away. 'It was you I came to see.'

He recognized at once the fact that she was in no humour for trivialities. He gave a brief order to the waiters, waved them away and leaned towards her.

'You can command me,' he assured her. 'My time is yours.'

She drew a little sigh of relief. For a moment her little white fingers rested upon his strong brown hand, the tenseness passed from her manner, it was as though she found something composing in his strength.

'I have been travelling for forty-eight hours,' she said, speaking under her breath, 'and I had an escape, a very narrow escape, in Belgium. You do not want to understand everything, do you?'

'Nothing more than you choose,' he replied. 'I am your Man Friday.'

'Listen, then. Your car—it is in order?'

'Perfect. I came up from Bath the day before yesterday—sixty miles on the level and never changed speeds.'

'How long would it take you to get me down to the east coast?' she asked eagerly.

'What part?'

She hesitated.

'A small place called Blakeney, between Sheringham and Wells.'

He figured it out.

'Let me see,' he said,—'two hours to Newmarket, two more to Fakenham, saving a little on both runs if we escaped a puncture—say four hours and a half, Suzanne.'

'And your car?'

'In the garage, five minutes away in a taxicab.'

She breathed another sigh of relief.

'Now I shall eat some luncheon,' she declared. 'You will not mind if we commit ourselves to rather a wild-goose adventure?'

'I shall enjoy it immensely,' he assured her, 'if one can use such a word at all these days.'

He ordered some wine and watched the colour come back to her cheeks. Towards the end of the meal, however, she glanced often at the clock. He read her thoughts, signed his bill and stood up.

'I am going upstairs to my room for a moment,' she said briskly. 'Will you have a taxicab waiting?'

'Of course!'

She was gone barely ten minutes. When she came down she carried a small travelling case and wore a thick veil. He hurried her into the taxi, drove to the garage, and in less than half-an-hour London lay behind them, and the car was gathering speed at every moment. They passed through Finchley and Potter's Bar, slowed up through St. Albans, and settled down at racing speed, northwards. Suzanne opened her eyes.

'I am having a delicious rest,' she murmured.

'Where would you like some tea?' he inquired.

'Not yet. Push on as far as you can,' she begged. 'What time shall we reach Fakenham?'

He glanced at the clock on the splashboard.

'If you really like to run right through,' he said, 'you shall be there by six o'clock.'

She patted the hand which gripped the steering wheel.

'You dear person!' she exclaimed softly. 'Now I close my eyes again. I think I will sleep a little. Until I reached my rooms at twelve o'clock to-day I had not had my clothes off for two days. This air and the rest are wonderful.'

She settled back in her place and he touched the accelerator with his foot. Through Stevenage and Baldock, across the great open spaces to Royston, at sixty miles an hour to Newmarket, up the hill, along the Norwich road, then round to the left to Brandon, across the miles of heath with the stunted pine trees and miles of heather, into the more luxurious pastoral country of eastern Norfolk. It was half-past five when they crossed Fakenham Common and crept through the narrow streets of the old-fashioned town. He turned to look at her. She was still sleeping. She woke, however, as the car slackened speed.

'Where are we?' she asked.

'Fakenham,' he told her, 'with half-an-hour to spare. It's just half-past five.'

'You wonderful person,' she sighed, shaking herself free from the rugs.

They drew up in the archway 01 the hotel and made their way up the outside stairs into the old-fashioned coffee-room. She drank tea and toyed with her bread and butter absently. She looked continually out of the window, seawards.

'It is a wonderful day,' she said thoughtfully. 'There is no wind at all. They might come even before the time.'

He made her light a cigarette, followed her example, and in a few minutes they were again in the car. Half-an-hour later they looked down upon the quaint, old-world village of Blakeney, set amidst the marshlands, and beyond, the open sea. Suzanne was all alertness now and sat up by his side, gazing eagerly towards the line of white breakers. Suddenly, with a warning hoot, a long, grey car which had come up noiselessly behind them, swept past at a great speed. Suzanne gave a little exclamation.

'It is the car, I am sure!' she declared. 'It has come to meet him! All that I was told is true.'

'It's some car, all right,' Lavendale remarked, 'but I wouldn't have taken his dust as quietly as this if I'd heard him coming.'

She laughed at him.

'That car,' she said, 'is bound on the same errand that we are. It is on its way to Blakeney to meet the same passenger.'

'Well, we're in time, anyway,' was his only comment.

They slackened speed as they turned into the long, narrow street. About half-way down, the car in front of them was stopped by a soldier with drawn bayonet. A non-commissioned officer by the side was talking to the driver. Close at hand, a man in civilian clothes was lounging in front of what seemed to be the guardroom. Suzanne clutched her companion's arm in excitement.

'Ambrose!' she exclaimed. 'That's Major Elwell—the man in mufti, I mean! He is one of the chiefs of the English Secret Service.'

'I shall have to know a little more about this before I can catch on,' Lavendale confessed.

He brought his car slowly up behind the other one. The driver had raised his goggles and was seated in an impassive attitude whilst his license was being examined. Presently the little green book was returned to him and he moved slowly down the village street. Lavendale's license was inspected in the same fashion, after which they, too, followed down the village street, which terminated abruptly in a small dock, reached by an arm of the sea. Lavendale turned his car into the gateway of the inn, and together, a few moments later, they strolled down to the harbour. Only a thin stream of water covered the bottom of the estuary, scarcely enough to float a rowing boat, and one or two sailing barques were lying high and dry upon the mud. The stranger, who had drawn up his car by the side of the wall, was standing looking out seaward through a pair of field-glasses. Lavendale gazed across the marshes in the same direction, doubtfully.

'Say, you don't expect any ship that could cross the North Sea to come into dock here, do you?' he asked.

She nodded.

'Quite a large ship could come up at high tide,' she explained, 'but to-night they will not wait for the deep water. They will anchor outside and sail up in a smaller boat. Come for a walk a little way. That man is watching us.'

They strolled along a sandy lane, through a gate on the left opening on to the marshes. It was a grey and sombre evening, strangely still, colourless alike on sea and land and sky. A thin handful of cattle was stretched across the dyke-riven plain, a crowd of seagulls flapped their wings wearily overhead. Everywhere else an intense and almost mournful silence prevailed. Suzanne climbed to the top of one of the dykes and looked intently seaward.

'You see!' she exclaimed, pointing.

A small boat was anchored at the opening of the estuary. Beyond, almost on the horizon, was a thin line of smoke.

'They will not wait for the tide,' she told him, 'not the full tide, that is. They will come up as soon as that sailing boat can make the passage.'

'And who,' Lavendale inquired, 'will be the passenger?'

Her eyes flashed for a moment.

'He will be the man,' she said solemnly, 'who seeks to destroy France.' ...

They wandered a little way further out into the marshland. The air seemed to possess a peculiar saltiness—even in that slightly moving breeze they could feel the brackish taste upon their lips. They watched the tidal way grow deeper every minute. On either side of them the narrow dykes and curving waterways grew fuller and fuller with the tendrils of the sea. About a mile from the distant coast-line the steamer seemed to have come to an anchor, and the white-sailed boat was fluttering about her. Suzanne took Lavendale's arm. He could feel that she was trembling.

'Look here,' he begged, 'tell me a little more of what is going to happen?'

'Somebody will be landed from that steamer,' she said. 'They will come up here, get into the motor-car and start for London. That some one will be empowered to put certain propositions before the Russian Ambassador here, which he in his turn can convey to the Tsar in code. Those propositions will be for a peace which will exclude my country and yours, which will give Russia, temporarily defeated, the terms of a conquering nation.'

He laughed a little contemptuously.

'You don't need to worry, child,' he assured her. 'Russia isn't going to cave in yet awhile.'

'Not in any ordinary fashion,' she replied, 'but one lives in dread of some terrible disaster, and then—— These terms, they say, are to be left over for a month. Think of the temptation—all the fruits of victory offered in the very blackest moment of despair. Look!'

She pointed to the mouth of the river. The white-sailed boat was already commencing the passage of the estuary.

'Come,' she exclaimed, 'we must get back.'

They hurried across the marsh, finding their way with more difficulty now owing to the inward sweep of the tide, filling the narrow places with the soft swirl of salt-water. When they reached the raised path by the side of the estuary, the sailing boat was almost by their side. A man was seated in the stern, muffled up in an overcoat and wearing a tweed cap.

'There he is,' she murmured.

Lavendale glanced at the man in a puzzled fashion. Just at that moment the latter turned his head. He was dark, clean-shaven, and slightly built.

'Something rather familiar about him,' Lavendale muttered. 'You don't know his name?'

She shook her head.

'Wait,' she begged.

They reached the dock just as the boat was drawing up to the quay-side.

'Get out the car, please,' Suzanne directed, 'and drive slowly up the street, just past the guardroom. Wait there as though we had been stopped again.'

Lavendale obeyed. This time, as they drew up, Major Elwell leaned over the front of the car.

'He is here, I understand, Miss de Freyne,' he said softly. 'Are you going to stay? There may be a little trouble.'

She laughed derisively.

'This is Mr. Lavendale,' she whispered. 'He will take care of me, Major Elwell.'

The latter looked keenly at Lavendale and nodded.

'It's a queer piece of business, this,' he observed. 'Maybe our information is all wrong, after all.'

The other car came gliding up the village street and was brought to a standstill only a foot behind them. The driver addressed the sergeant almost angrily.

'I showed you my license a few minutes ago,' he protested. 'What's that other car doing ahead, blocking up the way?'

Lavendale drew slightly on one side. A soldier, with fixed bayonet, slipped into the little space between the two cars. Major Elwell turned towards the passenger.

'Sorry to trouble you, sir,' he said, 'but I must ask you to step inside the guardroom for a moment.'

'What do you want with me?' was the quick reply.

'You've landed from a steamer here, rather an exceptional thing to do anyway,' Major Elwell explained. 'There are just a few questions we should like to ask.'

'I'm an American citizen,' the other declared. 'I have my passport here. I can land where I choose.'

'In ordinary times, without a doubt,' the Major replied smoothly. 'Just now, I am sorry to be troublesome, but there are some new enactments which have to be considered. We shall have to ask you to give up anything you may have in the way of correspondence, for instance, to be censored.'

There was a moment's silence. The face of the man in the car had suddenly become tense. Lavendale, who had been looking around, gave a little start.

'Why, it's Johnson!' he exclaimed—'Leonard Johnson! You remember me, don't you—Lavendale?'

The man in the car nodded eagerly.

'Of course!' he assented. 'Look here, if you've any pull in these parts, I wish you'd persuade this officious gentleman to let me go on quickly. I'm in a hurry to reach London.'

'I'm afraid I can't,' Lavendale regretted. 'I'm hung up myself for some piffling reason. Where have you come from?'

'Holland,' was the brief reply.

'If you are really in a hurry, sir,' Major Elwell intervened politely,' you are only wasting time by this discussion with your friend. Before you proceed, you will have to come into the guardroom with me.'

'I'm damned if I do!' Mr. Johnson replied. 'If you lay hands on me, I'll report the whole affair at the Embassy directly I arrive in London. I'm well enough known there, and they'll tell you that I am in the American Embassy at Berlin.'

Lavendale shook his head gently.

'Not at the present moment, I think, Johnson,' he remarked. 'I'll answer for it, though, that you are a reputable American citizen.'

'My instructions are entirely independent of your nationality,' Major Elwell said firmly. 'I must trouble you to descend at once.'

There was scarcely a whisper, scarcely even a glance between the two men in the hindmost car. Action seemed to be entirely spontaneous. Their car, which had moved perhaps a foot or so back while they were talking, as though the brakes had failed to hold, was suddenly swung to the right. The front wing caught the soldier who was standing on guard, and the car, plunging forward with one wheel upon the pavement, threw him off his balance. He reeled back against the wall, and almost before they could realize what had happened, the car was tearing up the hill. The sergeant snatched a rifle from one of the men but Major Elwell stretched out his hand.

'We don't want that!' he exclaimed. 'Telephone at once to all the places en route to London, car number LC 3221. Can you make any sort of speed, Mr. Lavendale?'

'Jump in,' was the grim reply. 'You'll soon see.'

They dashed up the hill, travelling almost at the same speed as the other car. As they passed the church they saw it a speck in the distance, climbing the next hill. Lavendale slipped in his fourth speed.

'Thank God for the dust!' he muttered. 'We shall see which way they go. Hold on, Suzanne. We'll have to take risks.'

The air rushed past them. The finger of the spedometer crept up from thirty to fifty and sixty miles an hour. They swung round the corner, and through a tiny village, a cloud of dust rising behind, heedless of the curses shouted after them by the irate foot passengers.

'He's gone to the right,' Lavendale announced. 'That's Letheringsett. He'll leave the London road, though, if he can.'

'He'll try to give you the slip,' Major Elwell remarked, 'and take the train from somewhere.'

Lavendale smiled. The finger in front of them was still creeping upwards. They missed a hay wagon by a few inches. The pillar of dust in front of them grew nearer.

'We'll shepherd him into Fakenham,' Lavendale muttered. 'I could catch him now, if I wanted. They'll have had the message there, though.'

They skirted Letheringsett, up the hill, round corner after corner, through Thursford, with barely a hundred yards dividing them. Once, at some cross-roads, the car in front seemed to hesitate and they shot up to within fifty yards. The light now was becoming bad. There were little patches of shadow where the trees overhung the road.

'They're giving it up!' Lavendale exclaimed. 'By Jove, we've got them!'

He pointed forward. The road running into Fakenham narrowed. A line of three soldiers stood across the thoroughfare. With a grinding of brakes and ponderous swaying of the foremost car, the chase was over. Mr. Leonard Johnson descended, shaking the dust from his coat.

'Following me?' he asked Lavendale sarcastically.

Major Elwell's hand fell upon his shoulder.

'We're not meaning to lose sight of you again just yet, sir,' he said.

'You know what risk you run in interfering with an American citizen?' the other demanded.

'Perfectly,' Major Elwell replied.

'You don't, that's certain, or you wouldn't attempt it,' Johnson snapped. 'However, we can't talk in the street. I'll get into your car and go on to the inn with you.'

They drove on to the Crown Inn, mounted the outside staircase, Lavendale in front and Major Elwell bringing up the rear. The coffee-room was empty. They rang for refreshments and dismissed the waiter. Johnson threw back his overcoat.

'Now, let's have this out,' he began truculently, addressing Major Elwell. 'Who the mischief are you, and what do you mean by following me like this?'

'I am censor for the neighbourhood in which you landed from Holland, Mr. Johnson,' was the quiet reply. 'Your present position is entirely the result of your own injudicious behaviour.'

'What exactly do you want?' Johnson demanded.

'After your attempts to escape,' Major Elwell announced, 'I shall be compelled to search you.'

Johnson drew a revolver from his pocket. His manner remained bellicose.

'Look here,' he said, 'if you're looking for trouble you can have it. I don't recognize the right of anybody to interfere with my movements.'

Major Elwell strolled slowly across the room to where Johnson was standing, looking all the time down the muzzle of the outstretched revolver.

'One moment, Mr. Johnson,' he said. 'Do you mind glancing out of this window? No, you can keep your weapon—I've no designs on that. Just look down into the street.'

Johnson did as he was bidden. Half a dozen soldiers were lined up outside the entrance.

'Then out of the door, if you please,' the Major further suggested.

He held it open. At the bottom of the stairs a sentry was standing with drawn bayonet. Johnson stared at him for a moment. Then he turned abruptly away.

'Look here,' he said hoarsely, 'this censor business don't go with me. You're lying!'

'Perhaps so,' Major Elwell admitted smoothly, 'and so are you. You mentioned, I think, that you had been in the American Embassy at Berlin. You omitted to mention, however, that you have since joined the German Secret Service. As that fact is well-known to us, you can understand, I dare say, why we regard this landing of yours upon a lonely part of the coast with some—shall I say suspicion?'

Johnson stood very still for a moment. He seemed to be thinking deeply.

'This censorship of yours is a bluff, I suppose,' he muttered.

'Amongst many other positions,' Major Elwell admitted, 'I also hold a somewhat important place in the English Secret Service. You have, I trust, one of the first qualifications for useful service in your profession—you are able to recognize the inevitable? You are face to face with it now.'

There was a brief silence. Johnson was standing at the window with his hands behind him. Presently he turned around.

'Very well,' he pronounced curtly, 'you've got me fairly enough. Go ahead.'

'You see,' Major Elwell explained, 'you might, under the present laws, be treated as an ordinary indiscreet traveller—or as a spy. Better hand over everything you are carrying.'

Johnson opened his coat pocket and threw a few letters and a pocket-book upon the table. Major Elwell glanced them through and sighed. Then he turned towards Suzanne.

'If you would give us a couple of minutes, please,' he begged.

Lavendale led her out into the yard. In a few minutes the door behind them was thrown open. The Major was standing at the top of the steps.

'Where's the car?' he shouted—'the car they came in?'

Lavendale looked down the yard and dashed into the street.

'Where's the other car?' he asked one of the soldiers on guard.

'No instructions to detain it, sir,' the man replied. 'The chauffeur drove it to the garage to fill up with petrol.'

They ran across the street in a little procession. The man in charge of the place stared at them, a little dazed.

'Car came in about ten minutes ago—a great Delauney-Belleville,' he informed them. 'She filled up and started off for London.'

Major Elwell turned towards Lavendale and laughed hardly.

'That fellow's first job, he muttered, 'and he's done us in! The documents he was carrying are in that car!'

*****

Major Elwell spent the next hour in the telegraph office whilst Lavendale and Suzanne raced southwards. More than once they had news of the car of which they were in pursuit. At Brandon it was only twenty minutes ahead, and at Newmarket they learnt that the driver had called at the station, found there was no train for an hour and continued his journey. From Newmarket, through Six-Mile-Bottom and onwards, they touched seventy miles an hour, and even Suzanne shivered a little in her seat. At the Royston turn the sparks flew upwards through the grey light as Lavendale's brakes bit their way home.

'Two ways to London here,' he muttered. 'Wait.'

He took a little electric torch from his pocket and stooped down in the road. In less than a dozen seconds he was back in the driving seat.

'By Royston,' he whispered. 'I fancy, somehow, we are gaining on him.'

They tore onwards along the narrow but lonelier road. Once, on a distant hillside far in front, they caught the flash of a light. Lavendale gave a little whoop of triumph.

'We shall get him,' he cried fiercely. 'We've twenty miles of road like this to Royston.'

The excitement of the chase began to tell on both of them. Suzanne, sitting close to the side of the car, leaned a little forward, her eyes bright, her hair wind-tossed, her cheeks flushed, breathless all the time with the lashing of their speed-made wind. Lavendale sat like a figure of wood, leaning a little over his wheel, his hands rigid, his whole frame tense with the strain. Once more they saw the light, this time a little nearer. Then they skidded crossing an unexpected railway track, took a few seconds to right themselves, and the light shot ahead. They passed through Royston and shot up the hill, scarcely slackening speed. It was a little before moonlight now, and the heath stretching away on their left seemed like some silent and frozen sea on which the mists rested lightly. Suddenly a little cry broke from Lavendale's lips, his foot crushed down upon the brakes. In front of them, by the side of the road, was the other car, disabled, its left wheel missing, the driving seat empty. They came to a standstill within a few feet of it and Lavendale leapt lightly out. Lying with his head upon the grass was the driver. Lavendale bent rapidly over him.

'The front wheel must have shot off and pitched him forward,' he explained to Suzanne. 'I'm afraid he is hurt. You'd better go and sit in the car.'

Then the woman he had seen nothing of blazed out from the girl by his side.

'Do not be foolish,' she cried fiercely. 'He is alive, is he not? Quick! Search him!'

Lavendale for a moment was staggered. He was feeling for the man's heart.

'What is the life or death of such as he!' she continued, almost savagely. 'Search him, I say!'

Lavendale obeyed her, a little dazed. There was a license, a newspaper of that morning's date, a few garage receipts for petrol, a handkerchief, a penknife and a large cigarette case—not another thing. She pushed him on one side while she felt his body carefully. The man opened his eyes, groaning.

'My leg!' he muttered.

Lavendale stood up.

'I think that's all that's the matter with him,' he pronounced—'fracture of the leg. We'd better take him back to the hospital.'

'Leave him alone,' she ordered. 'Come here with me at once.'

Lavendale obeyed mutely. She sprang up into the dismantled car and began feeling the cushions.

'Look in the pockets,' she directed.

Lavendale turned them inside out. There were maps, a contour book, an automobile handbook, more garage receipts, an odd glove—nothing of interest. Suddenly Suzanne gave a little cry. She bent closer over the driving cushion, pulled at a little hidden tab, opened it. There reposed a letter in a thick white envelope, the letter of their quest. Lavendale flashed his electric torch upon it. It was addressed in plain characters:—

To His Excellency.

He thrust it into his pocket.

'Look here,' he insisted, 'we've found what we want. We must see about that man now.'

They lifted him into their car and drove him back to the hospital. Lavendale left money, called at the police-station and gave information about the accident. Then they ran up to the hotel and stood side by side for a moment in the dimly-lit, stuffy coffee-room. He drew the letter from his pocket.

'Well?' he asked.

She glanced at the seal—huge and resplendent.

'It is only the first part of our task that is done,' she sighed, 'yet everything is ready for the second. That letter will be delivered. It is the answer we want.'

She took the letter and placed it in the small bag she was carrying.

'Some sandwiches, please,' she begged, 'and then London.'

*****

Twenty-four hours later they sat in her little sitting-room. Suzanne was restless and kept glancing at the clock, lighting cigarettes and throwing them away. Often she glanced at Lavendale, imperturbable, a little troubled.

'Why do you frown?' she demanded.

'I don't know,' he answered simply. 'This business has its dark side, you know. I was thinking of it from your point of view. You are going to open a friend's letter—that's what it comes to. You're on fire to see whether your friend, whom you should trust, is as honourable as you think him. It leaves an unpleasant flavour, you know.'

She came to a standstill before him.

'My friend,' she said, 'you have something yet to learn in our profession. It is this—honour and joy, conduct itself, idealism, all those things that make up the mesh of life, lose their significance to the man or woman who works for his country as I have done, as you have commenced to do. I am for France alone, and for France's sake I have no character. For France's sake I have sent a dummy messenger to the Prince. For France's sake I shall open the reply. It may tell me everything, it may tell me nothing, but one must be warned.'

There was a ring at the bell. A young man entered, closing the door behind him. Suzanne almost sprang towards him.

'You have the answer?' she cried.

The messenger bowed. Suzanne was suddenly calm. She tore open the long, thick envelope with trembling fingers. She peered inside for a moment, doubtfully. Then her whole face relaxed, her eyes flashed with joy. She held the envelope up over the table. A little stream of torn pieces of paper fell from it. Her eyes were moist as she watched them.

'It is the offer of our enemy,' she cried, 'and the answer of our ally! Some scraps of paper!'

CHAPTER VIII.
THE UNDENIABLE FORCE

Lavendale drew a deep sigh of content as he withdrew his eyes reluctantly from the glittering phantasmagoria of the city, stretching away below like a fire-spangled carpet. He leaned back in his chair and raised his glass to his lips.

'No doubt about my being an American born, Moreton,' he observed. 'The first night in New York is always a real home-coming to me. And this is New York, isn't it?' he went on, musingly, 'city of steel and iron, typical, indescribable.'

Jim Moreton, an erstwhile college friend and now a prosperous lawyer, nodded sympathetically.

'We are right in the heart of things here,' he assented. 'Nothing like a roof garden round about Broadway, to see us at home. I wonder whether you noticed any change?' he went on. 'They tell us that we get more European every year in our love of pleasure and luxury.'

Lavendale glanced around at the many little groups dining on the twenty-eighth storey of a famous hotel, under the light of the big, yellow moon. The table illuminations, and the row of electric lights which ran along the parapet, seemed strangely insignificant. Everywhere was a loud murmur of conversation, punctuated by much feminine laughter, the incessant popping of corks, the music of the not too insistent band.

'I tell you, Jimmy,' he confided, leaning forward towards his friend, 'to look into the faces of these people is the greatest relief I have known for twelve months. Just at first, when war broke out, one didn't notice much change, in England especially, but latterly there has been no mistaking it. Wherever you went, in the streets or the restaurants, you could see the writing in the faces of the people, a sort of dumb repression of feeling, just as though they were trying to get through the task of every-day life because they had to, eating and drinking because they had to, talking, amusing themselves, even, with an absent feverishness all the time—unnatural. I tell you it's like being in some sort of a dream to be in London or Paris to-day. It's only to-night I've felt myself back amongst real men and women again, and it's good.'

Moreton nodded understandingly.

'A fellow was writing something of the sort in one of the Sunday papers last week,' he remarked. 'Over here, of course, the whole thing to us is simply pictorial. We don't realize or appreciate what is happening. We can't.'

'And yet some day,' Lavendale sighed, 'we shall have to go through it ourselves.'

'One of your Harvard theories cropping up again!'

'It's more than a theory now—it's a certainty,' Lavendale insisted. 'One doesn't need to brood, though. There's plenty of real life buzzing around us all the time. Do you know why I sent you that wireless, Jim?'

'Not an idea on earth,' the other admitted. 'I guess I was conceited enough to hope that you wanted to see me again.'

'That's so, anyway,' Lavendale assured him, 'and you know it, but apart from that I want you to do something for me. I want to meet your uncle.'

'I'll do what I can,' Moreton promised, a little dubiously. 'He isn't the easiest person to get at, as you know.'

'Where is he now?' Lavendale inquired.

'I haven't had a line from him or my aunt for months,' Moreton replied, 'but the papers say he is coming to New York to-night.'

'Is there anything in these sensational reports about his new discovery?' Lavendale asked eagerly.

'I shouldn't be surprised,' the other confessed. 'There is no doubt that he is giving up his laboratories and closing down in the country. He told me himself, last time I saw him, that the thing he'd been working at, off and on, for the last thirty years, was in his hands at last, perfect. He's through with inventing—that's how he put it to me. He is going to spend the rest of his days reading dime novels in the mornings and visiting cinemas in the afternoons—says his brain's tired.'

'I shouldn't wonder at that,' Lavendale observed. 'He was seventy-two last year, wasn't he? I wonder how long he'll keep his word, though.'

'He seems in earnest. He has been very cranky lately, and they were all terrified down at Lakeside that he'd blow the whole place up.'

'You don't know any particulars about this last invention, I suppose?'

'If I did,' Moreton declared with a little laugh, 'I could have had my weight in dollars from the newspaper men alone. No, I know nothing whatever about it. All I can promise is that I'll take you up to Riverside Drive and do my best to boost you in. Now tell me what you've been doing with yourself this year, Ambrose? You've left the Diplomatic Service, haven't you?'

'Not altogether. I have a sort of unofficial position at the Embassy, perhaps as important as my last one, only not quite so prominent.'

'Still as great a scaremonger as ever? Do you remember those discussions you used to start at the debating society?'

'I remember them all right,' Lavendale assented grimly, 'and since you ask me the question, let me tell you this, Jim. I've lived, as you know, during the last seven years in the diplomatic atmosphere of Paris, of London and Berlin. I tell you soberly that anything I felt and believed in those days, I feel and believe twice as strongly to-day. Just look over your left shoulder, Jimmy. Isn't that rather a queer-looking couple for a fashionable roof-garden!'

Moreton turned a little lazily around. An elderly man and woman who had just entered were being shown to an adjacent table. The man was apparently of some seventy years of age, his morning clothes were of old-fashioned cut and he wore only a little wisp of black tie. His grey beard was cut in the fashion of a century ago, his bushy hair was long and unkempt. His companion, who seemed but a few years younger, wore the simplest of dark travelling clothes, some jet jewellery, a huge cameo brooch fastened a shawl at her throat and she carried a leather handbag.

'Don't they look as though they'd come out of the ark!' Lavendale murmured.

Moreton had risen slowly to his feet.

'Queer thing that you should spot them, Ambrose,' he remarked. 'This is what you might call something of a coincidence.'

'You don't mean to say that you know them?'

Jim Moreton nodded.

'My Uncle Ned and my Aunt Bessie,' he said. 'I must go and speak to them.'

He crossed towards the elderly couple, shook hands with the man, who greeted him cordially enough, and submitted to an embrace from the lady. Lavendale could hear, every now and then, scraps of their conversation. Towards its close, his friend turned and beckoned to him. Lavendale, who had been eagerly awaiting a summons, rose at once and approached the trio.

'Aunt,' Moreton explained, laying his hand upon his friend's shoulder, 'this is Mr. Ambrose Lavendale, a graduate of my year at Harvard. Uncle, Lavendale has just returned from Europe and he was talking to me about you. He is like the rest of us, tremendously interested in what all the world is saying about you and your latest discovery.'

Lavendale shook hands with the elderly couple, who greeted him kindly.

'Discovery, eh?' Mr. Moreton observed jocularly.

'That does seem rather an inadequate word,' Lavendale admitted. 'I think one of your own newspapers here declared that you had learnt how to bottle up the lightnings, to— —'

'Oh, those damned papers!' Mr. Moreton exclaimed irritably. 'Don't talk to me about them, young fellow.'

'I would much rather talk to you about what they are aiming at,' Lavendale said simply. 'Are you going to give any demonstration, sir—I mean, of course, to the scientific world?'

The inventor glanced up at his questioner with a little twinkle in his hard, blue eyes.

'Say, you've some nerve, young fellow!' he declared amiably. 'However, I am very fond of my nephew here, and if you're a friend of

Jim's you shall be one of a very select company to-morrow morning. The scientific world can wait, but I am going to set the minds of the newspaper people at rest. I am going to show them what I can do. I was thinking of asking you, any way, Jim,' he went on, 'and you can bring your friend with you. Twelve o'clock at Riverside Drive.'

The two young men were both profuse in their thanks. Mr. Moreton waved them away. 'There will be just three or four newspaper men,' he continued—'I put the names of the principal papers into a bottle and drew lots; the reporters who came down to Jersey State agreed to that—you two, your aunt and a young lady. You can go and finish your dinner now, boys. Your aunt and I, Jim, are going on to a cinema afterwards. We're going to make a real night of it.'

The two young men shook hands and made their adieux. As soon as they had resumed their places, Lavendale leaned across the table towards his friend with glowing face.

'Jimmy, you're a brick,' he declared. 'We'll have another bottle on the strength of this. The very night I arrive, too! Whoever heard of such luck! I don't suppose I should ever have got within a hundred yards of him but for you.'

'He's a shy old bird,' Moreton admitted. 'We certainly were in luck to-night though.'

'I wonder who the girl is who's going to be there,' Lavendale remarked idly.

His eyes had suddenly strayed once more over the brilliant yet uneasy panorama of flashing lights, huge buildings, the throbbing and clanging of cars across the distant line of the river to the blue spaces beyond. The leader of the little orchestra behind was playing a familiar waltz. Suzanne and he had danced it together one night in London. He was for a moment oblivious of the whole gamut of his surroundings. The world closed in upon him. He heard her voice, felt the touch of her fingers, saw a gleam of the tenderness which sometimes flashed out from beneath the suffering of her eyes. His friend glanced at him in wonder. It was the insistent voice of a waiter which brought him back from his reverie.

'French or Turkish coffee, sir?'

Lavendale made a heedless choice and climbed down to the present.

'Way back somewhere, weren't you?' Jim Moreton remarked. His friend nodded.

'I have left behind a great deal that one remembers.'

*****

At a few minutes before twelve on the following morning, Lavendale and his friend were conducted by a coloured butler across a very magnificent entrance hall of black and white marble, strewn with wonderful rugs, through several suites of reception rooms, and out on to a broad stone piazza, at the back of Mr. Moreton's mansion in Riverside Drive. It was here that Lavendale received one of the surprises of his life. Mr. and Mrs. Moreton were reclining in low wicker chairs, and between them, a miracle of daintiness in her white linen costume and plain black hat, was—Suzanne. Lavendale forget his manners, forgot the tremendous interest of his visit, forgot everything else in the world. He stood quite still for a moment. Then he strode forward with outstretched hands and a very visible gladness in his face.

'Suzanne!' he exclaimed. 'Why, how wonderful!'

She laughed at him gaily as she accepted his greeting. There was some response to his joy shining out of her eyes, but it was obvious that his presence was less of a surprise to her.

'You did not know that I was here?' she asked. 'But why not? Men and women have travelled many times round the world before now to learn its secrets.'

Lavendale recovered a little of his self-possession. He shook hands with Mrs. Moreton, who was beaming placidly upon them, mutely approving of this unexpected romance. The great inventor turned him round by the shoulder and indicated four men of varying ages who formed the rest of the little company.

'I will not introduce you by name,' he said, 'but these four gentlemen, selected by lot, as I think I told you last night, represent the mightiest and holiest power on earth—the great, never-to-be-denied Press of America. They are here because, since the first rumour stole from my laboratory down in Jersey State that I had reached the end of my labours, I have been the victim of an incessant and turbulent siege, carried on relentlessly day by day—I might almost say hour by hour. For good reasons I desired to keep my discovery to myself a little longer, but I know that I am beaten, and these gentlemen, or rather the power which they represent, have been too many for me. My country household has been honeycombed with spies. My medical man, my gardener, the assistants in my laboratory, have every one of them been made the objects of subtle and repeated attempts at bribery. Young Mr. Lavendale, let me tell you this—the Press of America to-day is the one undeniable force. Look at them—my conquerors. I am going to present them to-day with my secret—not willingly, mind, but because, if I do not yield, they will continue to eat with me, to sleep with me and to walk with me, to plague my days and curse my nights. This young lady,' he continued, in an altered tone, 'came to me with a personal letter from my cousin, our Ambassador in Paris. You, Mr. Lavendale, are here as my nephew's friend. Now, if you are ready, I will proceed with the demonstration.'

The four men had risen to their feet. One of them, a well-set-up, handsome young fellow, shook hands with Lavendale.

'I was a year before you at Harvard, wasn't I?' he remarked. 'We think that Mr. Moreton is just a little hard upon us. We represent, to use his own words, the undeniable force, and to do it we have to forget that we are human, and persist. This may be very annoying to Mr. Moreton, but as a rule it is the world that benefits.'

The inventor, who had disappeared for a moment in the interior of the room which led out on to the piazza, suddenly stood upon the threshold. His face seemed to have become graver during the last few moments and he motioned them impatiently back to their places. Then, with a reel of what seemed to be fine wire in his hand, he made his way to the further end of the broad balcony which completely encircled the house, and carefully stretched a length of the wire from the edge of the building to the stone balustrade. As soon as he had accomplished this, he drew from his pockets what appeared to be a pair of black gloves of some spongy material, and a tiny instrument about the size of a lady's watch, which none of them could see. He drew on the gloves with great care, placed the instrument between the palms of his hands and turned to his nephew.

'Just ring the bell there, will you, Jimmy?' he directed.

The young man obeyed. The little group now were all standing up, their eyes fixed upon that strip of thin wire. Mr. Moreton slowly drew his palms together several times, pausing once to glance at the small instrument which lay concealed between them. Footsteps were heard approaching around the side of the house, and a coloured servant in livery, carrying a tray in his hand, appeared. He had no sooner set his foot upon the wire than he stopped short, gave a wild jump into the air, came down again, jumped again, and slowly, with the salver still in his hand, began to dance.

'Touch the bell,' the inventor ordered, in a voice which seemed tense with suppressed emotion.

His nephew obeyed at once and again there were footsteps. Another servant, carrying a chair, came round the corner, paused for a moment as though in amazement on perceiving the antics of his predecessor, stepped on to the wire, leapt into the air, and commenced to perform almost similar gyrations. Mr. Moreton's breath was coming fast and he seemed to be the victim of some peculiar emotion. This time he only glanced towards the bell, which his nephew pushed. Again there were footsteps. A third servant, with a box of cigars, appeared, gave a little exclamation at the extraordinary sight before him, stepped forward on to the wire, leapt up till his head almost touched the sloping portico, and commenced throwing the cigars into the air and catching them. Mr. Moreton glanced from the three performers towards his little audience. The expression on their faces was absolutely indescribable. Meanwhile, the dancing of the three men in livery became more rapid. The man with the salver and glasses began throwing them into the air and catching them again, the servant on the outside was now occupied in balancing a cigar on the tip of his nose, while his neighbour on the right was twirling the wicker chair which he had been carrying, on the point of his forefinger. Mr. Moreton stretched out his hand towards the spellbound, stupefied little company.

'The Hamlin Trio, gentlemen, of jugglers and dancers, imported from the Winter Gardens at great expense for your entertainment! Good morning!'

With one bound he was through the window. They heard the bolt slipped into its place. From behind the glass he turned and waved his hand to the newspaper men. Then he disappeared.

'Spoofed, my God!' the journalist who had spoken to Lavendale, exclaimed.

For a single moment they all looked at one another. The trio of entertainers were redoubling now their efforts. There was a roar of laughter.

'The joke's on us,' one of the other newspaper men admitted candidly, 'but what a story! We'd better get along and write it, you fellows,' he added, 'before they have it up against us.'

'Is there any chance,' a third man inquired, 'of Mr. Moreton talking to us reasonably?'

His wife beamed placidly upon them.

'Not one chance in this life,' she assured them. 'If you knew the language poor dear Ned has used about you gentlemen of the Press worrying him down at Lakeside during the last few months, you'd only wonder that he has let you off so lightly.'

'Then perhaps,' Lavendale's acquaintance suggested, 'we'd better be getting along.'

The Hamlin Trio, at the other end of the piazza, suddenly ceased their labours, made a collective bow and disappeared. The newspaper men still lingered, looking longingly at the bolted window. Mrs. Moreton shook her head.

'Just leave him alone for a little time,' she begged. 'He has got a down on you newspaper gentlemen, and the way they worried him down at New Jersey has pretty well driven him crazy. Don't try him any more this morning, if you please,' she persisted. 'It's my belief this little joke he's played on you kept him out of the hospital.'

The silvery-haired old lady, with her earnest eyes and the little quaver in her tone, triumphed. The little company reluctantly dispersed. Lavendale and Suzanne were on the point of following the others when a head was thrust cautiously out of a window on the second storey of the house.

'Has the Press of the United States departed?' Mr. Moreton inquired.

'They've all gone, dear,' his wife called out soothingly.

'Then bring the others in to luncheon,' Mr. Moreton invited.

'I'll bring them in right away,' Mrs. Moreton promised. 'Say, that's a good sign, young people,' she added, turning to them cheerfully. 'He has hated the sight of company lately, but I did feel real uncomfortable at sending you away without any offer of hospitality. He has locked this window fast enough,' she added, trying it, 'but come right along with me and I'll show you another way in.'

They followed her along the piazza. Lavendale and Suzanne fell a little way behind. It was their first opportunity.

'How long have you been here?' he asked eagerly. 'What did you come for? Why didn't you let me know?'

'I have been in New York four days,' she told him. 'I was on the *City of Paris*. We passed you near Queenstown. As for the rest, I suppose I am here for the same reason that you are. Monsieur Senn, the great electrician, has been working on the same lines as Moreton for years, and he persuaded me to get a letter from the American Ambassador in Paris and come out here. I do not suppose, though, that it is any use. They say that Mr. Moreton is like you — American inventions for the American people.'

'I've wobbled once or twice,' he reminded her.

'Of course, there's always a chance,' she murmured.

'Say that you are glad to see me?' he begged.

She gave his hand a little squeeze. Then Mrs. Moreton turned round with a motherly smile.

'If you'll take your cocktail in the smoking-room with Jimmy, Mr. Lavendale,' she said, 'I'll look after Miss de Freyne.' ...

Luncheon was a meal of unexpected simplicity, served by a couple of trim waiting-maids in a magnificent apartment which overlooked the Hudson. Mr. Moreton was in high good-humour over his latest exploit, and they all indulged in speculations as to the nature of the stories which would appear in the evening editions. Underneath his hilarity, however, Lavendale more than once fancied that he noted signs of an immense tension. Sometimes, in the middle of a conversation, the great inventor would break off as though he had lost the thread of what he had been saying, and look uneasily, almost supplicatingly around him until some one supplied him with the context of his speech. Towards the end of the meal, after a brief silence, he turned with curious abruptness towards Lavendale.

'Say, you've come a long way to see nothing, young man,' he remarked.

'I have had the pleasure of meeting you, sir,' Lavendale replied politely, 'and, after all, I never believed the things they were saying in London.'

'What were they saying?' Mr. Moreton demanded brusquely.

'There was a report there when I left,' Lavendale answered, 'that you had learnt at last the secret of handling electricity by wireless, handling it, I mean, in destructive fashion.'

'Oh! they said that, did they?' Mr. Moreton observed, smiling to himself.

'To be absolutely exact,' Lavendale went on, 'they said that you had professed to discover it. A great scientific man whom I met only a few days before I left England, however—Sir Hubert Bowden—assured me that mine would be a wasted journey because the thing was impossible.'

A suddenly changed man sat in Mr. Moreton's place. The unhealthy pallor of his skin was disfigured by dark red, almost purple patches. His eyes were like glittering beads. He struck the table fiercely with his hairy fist.

'Bowden is an ass!' he exclaimed. 'He is an ignorant numskull, a dabbler, a blind follower in other men's footsteps. Impossible to me—Moreton?'

'My dear! My dear!' his wife murmured anxiously from the other end of the table.

The inventor turned to one of the servants.

'Telephone to the garage for the car to be here in ten minutes,' he ordered. 'I have had my little joke,' he went on, as the girl left the room. 'This afternoon we'll get to business.'

His fury seemed to pass away as suddenly as it had come. He ate and drank nervously but with apparent appetite. As soon as the meal was over he commenced smoking a black cigar, and, excusing himself rather abruptly, left the room.

'Do you suppose,' Lavendale asked his hostess, 'that he is really going to give us a demonstration?'

'I don't know,' she answered uneasily. 'I wish I could get him somewhere right away from every one who talks about inventions and electricity. You put his back up, you know, Mr. Lavendale. He was quite all right before you handed him that sort of challenge.'

'I am sorry,' Lavendale murmured mendaciously.

In a few minutes they received an urgent summons. They found Mr. Moreton waiting in a large, open car below. He had quite recovered his temper. His face, indeed, shone with the benign expression of a child on its way to a treat.

'Miss de Freyne and Mr. Lavendale, you can sit by my side,' he ordered. 'Jimmy, you get up in front. The man knows where to go.'

They swung round and in a few minutes turned into Central Park. At a spot where the road curved rather abruptly, the car came to a standstill. Mr. Moreton stepped out. From his pocket he drew a small skein of what seemed to be white silk, and a tiny instrument with a dial face and perforated with several holes.

'Hold that,' he directed Lavendale.

The latter obeyed. Mr. Moreton drew the thread of white silk backwards and forwards through one of the apertures in the instrument, the finger on the dial face mounting all the time from zero. When it reached a certain figure he drew it out, and, stooping down, stretched it across the path from the hedge to the curbstone. Then he glanced up and down and around the corner. The park was almost deserted and there were only a few loungers in sight. From the small bag which he had brought with him in the car, Mr. Moreton next produced a square black box with a handle in the side, and a pair of black indiarubber gloves which he hastily donned. Then, with the box in his hand, he turned the handle which protruded from its side. A queer, buzzing little sound came from the interior, a sound which, low though it was, thrilled Lavendale from its utter and mysterious novelty. It was a sound such as he had never imagined, a sound like the grumblings of belittled and imprisoned thunder. The finger on the dial moved slowly. When it had reached a certain point, Mr. Moreton paused. He clasped the machine tightly in his hands. The mutterings still continued, and from a tiny opening underneath came little flashes of blue fire. The inventor stepped into the car, motioning the others to follow him, and gave an order to the driver. They backed to a spot by the side of the road, about a hundred yards away from where the thread of white silk lay stretched across the pavement. Mr. Moreton gripped the instrument in his rubber-clad hand and leaned back in the car, his eyes fixed upon the corner. His expression had become calmer, almost seraphic.

'We shall see now,' he promised them, smiling, 'another land of dance. There is only one thing I should like to point out. The little instrument I hold in my hand now is adjusted to any distance up to two hundred yards. By turning the handle a dozen more times, the distance could be increased to a mile, and more in proportion. The length of my silk-covered wire is immaterial. It could stretch, if desired, from here to Broadway. Now watch.'

They all sat with their eyes fastened upon the corner of the pathway. A slight uneasiness which Lavendale in particular had felt, was almost banished by a thrilling sense of expectancy. Suddenly a portly figure appeared, a policeman whom they had passed soon after entering the park. He approached with his hands behind him, walking in ruminating fashion. Suddenly, as his foot touched the thread, he came to a halt. There was something unnatural in his momentarily statuesque attitude. Then, before their eyes he seemed to stiffen, fell like a log on his right side, with his head in the roadway. His helmet rolled a few feet away. The man remained motionless. Lavendale sprang to his feet but Mr. Moreton pushed him back.

'That is of no consequence,' he said softly. 'Wait for a moment.'

Lavendale even then would have obeyed his instinct and jumped from the car, but his limbs seemed powerless. A man and a girl, arm in arm, appeared round the corner. Suzanne stood up. A strange, hysterical impulse seized her and she tried to shout. Her voice sounded like the feeblest whimper. The two lovers, as their feet touched the thread, seemed suddenly to break off in their conversation. It was as though the words themselves were arrested upon their lips, as though all feeling and movement had become paralyzed. Then they, too, stiffened and fell in the same direction. A park-keeper, who had seen the collapse of the policeman, came running across the road, shouting all the time, and an automobile which had been crawling along, increased its speed and raced to the spot. Mr. Moreton touched a button in the instrument which he was holding. The thunder died away and the blue flashes ceased. Suzanne leaned back in the car; her cheeks were as pale as death. Lavendale bent over her.

'It's all right, Suzanne,' he assured her. 'Sit here while I go down. There is nothing wrong with those people really. It's just another of Mr. Moreton's little jokes.'

Nevertheless, when Lavendale's feet touched the ground he gave a little cry, for the earth seemed quaking around him. Mr. Moreton, who was walking by his side, patted him on the shoulder.

'Steady, my boy! Steady!' he said. 'You see, the whole of the earth between here and that little thread of white silk is heavily charged. You feel, don't you, as though the ground were rising up and were going to hit you in the chin. I've grown used to it. There goes poor Jimmy. Dear me, he hasn't the nerve of a chicken!'

Young Moreton fell over in a dead faint. Lavendale set his teeth and staggered on. A little crowd was already gathering around the three prostrate bodies as they drew near.

'You see,' Mr. Moreton explained reassuringly, 'I have broken the connection now. Nothing more will happen.'

'What of those three—the policeman, the man and the girl?' Lavendale faltered.

Mr. Moreton patted him on the back. They had reached now the outskirts of the little group.

'Theirs,' he said gravely, 'was the real dance. You have been fortunate, young man. Your journey from Europe has been worth while, after all. You have seen the Hamlin Trio in their Jugglers' Dance, and you have seen here in the sunshine, under the green trees, with all the dramatic environment possible, the greatest dance of all—the dance of death.'

Lavendale felt the blood once more flowing freely in his veins. He turned almost fiercely upon his companion as he pushed his way through the gathering crowd.

'You don't mean that they are really dead?' he cried.

'Even your wonderful friend Bowden,' Mr. Moreton assured him sweetly, 'could never wake a single beat in their hearts again.'

An ambulance had just glided up. A man who seemed to be a doctor rose to his feet, shaking the dust from his knees.

'These three people are dead,' he pronounced sombrely. 'The symptoms are inexplicable.'

He suddenly recognized Moreton, who held out his hand genially towards him.

'Dr. Praxton, is it not?' he remarked. 'It is very fortunate that I should have so reliable a witness upon the spot. I shall be obliged, doctor, if you will take the bodies of these fortunate people into your keeping and prepare a careful examination of their condition.'

'Do you know anything about their death?' the doctor asked.

The great inventor smiled in a superior fashion.

'Why, my dear fellow, yes!' he assented. 'I killed them. You see that little skein of what seems to be white silk? If a million people had trodden upon it, one after the other, or if I in my car had been twenty miles away, with my instrument properly regulated, there would still be a million dead lying here. I am Moreton—Ned Moreton, the inventor, you know, doctor. I can strip the universe of life, if I choose. I should have liked,' he added, glancing a little peevishly over his shoulder, 'the young lady to have seen this. I shall make a point of her coming on to the hospital.'

The doctor glanced meaningly at the two or three policemen who had forced their way to the front. They led Mr. Moreton back to the car, and a few minutes later he was driven off, seated between them, smoking a cigar, the picture of amiability. Suzanne and Lavendale found a taxicab and left the park by another exit. She sat close to him, clinging to his arm.

'Suzanne,' he whispered, 'can you be a woman now for the sake of the great things?'

She sat up by his side. Her face was marble white, but some latent force seemed to have asserted itself. She answered him steadily.

'Go on, Ambrose,' she begged. 'I can listen. Do not be afraid.'

'I have told this man,' he continued, 'to drive to the docks. The *Marabic* is sailing at five o'clock.'

She looked at him for a moment as though she failed to understand. His arm tightened around her.

'I have the instruments and a skein of the thread in my pocket,' he whispered.

A sudden light flashed in her eyes. She leaned over and kissed him firmly and deliberately upon the lips.

'You are a man, Ambrose,' she declared. 'Do not be afraid. We are allies, is it not so?'

'In this, yes!' he promised her....

Two hours later, as they moved slowly down the river, the tugs shrieking in front of them, and siren whistles blowing on every side, they examined for the first time, in the security of Lavendale's stateroom, their new treasures—the black, camera-like instrument, the smaller one, with its dial face, and a little skein of the white, silk-covered wire. They both gazed at them almost in stupefaction—harmless-looking objects, silent, dead things.

'Only think,' she whispered, clutching his arm, 'we have but to learn their secret and we can end the war!'

Lavendale hid them away and silently they stole up on deck. They heard the engines quicken their beat, saw the great buildings of the city fade into an evening mist. They saw the lights shoot out from the Statue of Liberty and felt the ocean breeze on their cheeks. They turned their faces eastwards. The apprehension of great things kept them silent. They faced the Unknown.

CHAPTER IX.
AN INTERRUPTED REVUE

Madame Félanie sat before the gaily-decorated mirror which swung upon her dressing table, contemplating the result of her maid's careful and strenuous attentions. Her dressing-room, during the many months of her great success, had become transformed into a little bower of luxury and comfort. A telephone stood at her elbow amongst a chaos of tortoiseshell-backed toilet articles. There was a soft green carpet upon the floor, a wonderful divan in the most comfortable corner, a few trifles of Empire furniture, an etching or so upon the wall. Madame Félanie was a clever woman and she understood the art of environment.

Her costume now for the second act of the brilliant revue in which her success had been almost phenomenal, was practically completed. She wore still a rose-coloured dressing-gown over garments not remarkable for their prodigality, and though the evening papers, a French novel, a little volume of poetry sent from the author, and a box of Russian cigarettes stood at her elbow, she still continued to gaze a little abstractedly at the reflection of her own features in the looking-glass. London had found her beautiful, seductive, vivacious. She was all of these. Her dark and beautifully-set eyes restrained their gleam of natural violet notwithstanding the encompassment of stage make-up. No rouge could conceal the pearly brilliancy of her complexion, no cake of powder the charming lines of her mouth. It was not at these things, however, that she looked. Her eyes were fixed steadily upon the roots of her blue-black hair, drawn back from her forehead in a manner peculiar to herself. She even raised the tiny magnifying glass on the table before her, to concentrate her regard, and there was in her face almost at that moment a shadow, as though some faint foreboding was hovering over her, even in these halcyon days of her great triumph.

She laid the magnifying glass down.

'It is impossible,' she murmured to herself, stretching out her hand for a cigarette.

There was a knock at the door. Her maid came softly in—an elderly woman in prim black, softly-shod and with the art of moving noiselessly. She carried a card in her hand, which she presented to her mistress.

'Madame,' she announced, 'this gentleman desires the favour of a word with you.'

Félanie stretched out her hand.

'You know so well, Marie,' she complained, 'that I receive here only those who need send no card. Give him my address, if it is a gentleman from the Press.'

'I thought madame would prefer to see this gentleman,' the maid said quietly.

Still with a queer reluctance, Félanie took the card into her white fingers. Before she glanced at it she knew very well what name she would find written there, and she hated the knowledge. The black letters stared up at her—

Mr. Ambrose Lavendale,
17 Sackville Street.

Félanie turned her head slowly and looked upwards at her maid. The woman's face, however, was blank.

'The gentleman is doubtless known to Mr. Wiltshaw,' the latter continued. 'He secured the entrée here without difficulty. He waits now in the passage.'

'You can show him in,' her mistress ordered.

There were a few seconds during which another woman looked into that gaily-hung mirror, and another reflection appeared there. The mouth was no longer seductive, but grim. The eyes were no longer insolent, half challenging conquest, half promising tenderness, but seemed, indeed, to have receded a little, to be filled with the shrinking light of fear. The transition was extraordinary and complete. Here sat a terrified woman, face to face with some evil thing!

Then there came a knock at the door. As with the touch of her fingers upon the switch the gloom of the room was changed into brilliant light, so Félanie almost miraculously recovered herself.

She swung round in her dainty revolving chair. Her lips, even, fell naturally and easily into the lines of her most seductive smile. What fear there was at the woman's heart showed itself no longer in her face.

'Monsieur Lavendale—Monsieur Ambrose Lavendale, is it not?' she added, with a momentary glance at the card. 'You wish to see me?

Lavendale came a little further into the room and bowed. At a glance from her mistress, the maid softly withdrew, closing the door. In his severely simple evening clothes, Lavendale seemed in that little room to be taller even than his six feet two. Félanie, who had risen to her feet, felt herself suddenly dominated.

'Madame,' Lavendale said, 'I have ventured to present myself in order to renew a very delightful acquaintance.'

She played the game bravely.

'But, monsieur,' she protested, 'I have not the pleasure of knowing you.'

He sighed.

'It is, alas! then, your memory, madame, which is at fault.'

'Or yours?' she queried softly.

He shook his head.

'Those who have had the privilege of knowing the lady who calls herself now Madame Félanie, could make no mistake.'

'Yet it seems,' she persisted, acknowledging his courtesy with a smile, 'that that is what has happened. You are gallant, monsieur, but there are so many of us upon the stage who resemble one another.'

He shook his head with a self-confidence which she hated.

'There is no man in this world,' he declared, 'who could fail to recognize Adèle Goetz, even under the guise of Madame Félanie. May I congratulate you upon your great success? Your revue, they tell me, will run for ever.'

'You are very kind,' she said, her knees beginning to tremble a little, 'but indeed you are mistaken. My name is Elaine Félanie. It is my own name. I came from the Odéon. I am so well-known in Paris. This lady of whom you speak perhaps resembled me.'

Lavendale did not for a moment reply. His face had become a shade graver, his grey eyes held hers.

'Is there, then, a reason, madame,' he asked, 'why Adèle Goetz preferred to disappear and Madame Félanie to rise from her ashes? Am I not one of those who could be trusted? My memories of Mademoiselle Adèle are too delightful for me to bear anything but good-will towards Madame Félanie.'

She stood for a moment quite still. Her brain was working quickly. After all, the man was an American. She looked at him a little doubtfully. He smiled—and she yielded. She gave him both her hands.

'Monsieur Ambrose,' she said, 'it can go on no longer. I thought myself an actress but you have conquered. You are my friend?'

'Your devoted friend,' he assured her.

'You can imagine, then, why here in England it is Elaine Félanie alone who exists?'

'Adèle Goetz, if I remember rightly,' he replied, 'was of German birth.'

She glanced almost nervously around her. He went on without pause.

'So far as that simple fact is concerned,' he continued, 'you will not—you need have no fear of my discretion.'

She gave him her hands again and this time there was more of invitation in her gesture.

'You were always kind to me,' she murmured. 'We shall see something of one another now, is it not so?'

He shook his head.

'Alas! no, madame,' he sighed. 'I am engaged to be married.'

'And mademoiselle is jealous?' she inquired, with a little pout.

'There is no woman in the world,' he told her, 'who would not be jealous of Madame Félanie.'

She laughed at him with something of her old gaiety, threw herself back in her chair and passed him the cigarettes.

'We have a few minutes longer, at least,' she pleaded, 'before we make our pathetic farewells. You have not lost the gift of saying pleasant things, Ambrose.'

'Nor you, Adèle, the art of inspiring them,' he replied.

'Oh, là, là!' she exclaimed lightly. 'Tell me of your life here in London? Tell me why you came to renew our acquaintance if it is to be only a matter of this one visit?'

He had refused her offer of a chair and the cigarette, still unlit, was between his fingers.

'Yes, I will tell you that,' he said. 'You read, without a doubt, of the sinking of the *Marabic*?'

She shrugged her shoulders.

'Who has talked of anything else in London these few days?'

'I was amongst the saved,' he continued, 'I and the young lady to whom I am engaged to be married. We were in the last boat that left the ship and lost everything except the clothes we stood up in. That circumstance has, to a certain extent, changed my outlook upon this struggle.'

There was the slightest of frowns upon her velvet brow. She waited. He had the air of one, however, who has concluded all he has to say. He turned towards the door. She stopped him with an imperative gesture.

'You have not given me the promise I desire—I demand?' she cried. 'Monsieur Ambrose, you will not leave me like this?'

'That promise,' he said gravely, 'is yours—conditionally.'

His departure was a little abrupt and her gesture to recall him too late. She sat for a moment thinking, a curious shadow upon her face. Then she touched the bell.

'Ask Monsieur Anders to spare me a moment,' she directed her maid.

There was a brief interval, then the sound of a cheerful whistling outside. The door was opened and Monsieur Anders himself appeared. He was a small man with a strangely-lined face, a mouth whose humour triumphed even over his plastic make-up. He was attired with great magnificence in the costume of a beau of the last century. His fingers glittered with rings, lace cuffs fell over his wrists and a little waft of peculiar perfume entered with him. It was not for nothing that for many years he had been considered upon the French stage the embodiment of a certain type of elegance.

'You have had a visitor, *chérie?*' he remarked.

'I have,' she replied. 'Shut the door.'

He obeyed at once. From outside came the voice of the stage carpenter, the occasional rumbling of scenery, the music of the orchestra, the murmur now and then of applause. The curtain was up upon a fresh scene in the revue.

'Mysterious?' Anders murmured.

Suddenly, even as the word passed his lips, apprehension seemed to seize him. He remained for a moment dumb and motionless. Then he, too, glanced around before he leaned towards her.

'It is trouble?'

'Perhaps not,' she answered. 'One cannot tell. A young American has been to see me. He is one of the few who would remember. We were friends in Paris nine years ago. He was a boy then, but, notwithstanding everything, he recognized me.'

'An American,' Anders muttered. 'Better that than an Englishman! Well?'

'He was serving his apprenticeship in the American Diplomatic Service in those days,' she went on. 'What he is doing now I do not know, except that he and the girl whom he is engaged to marry, were amongst survivors from the *Marabic*. He went out of his way to pay me a visit here, just to tell me that he recognized me, and he made it plain that although he is not an Englishman, he is in sympathy with them.'

'Did he threaten?' Anders asked quickly.

'No,' she replied, 'and yet he terrified me. He promised silence—conditionally.'

'Conditionally? How?'

'He left that for me to understand. I am still puzzled. He does not want to see me any more—he took pains to tell me that he was engaged to be married. Yet underneath his manner I seemed to discover a threat.'

Anders stood perfectly still for a moment. Underneath all the paint and make-up of his face, he was suddenly haggard.

'Is it worth it, Henri?' she faltered. 'Why not America at once, and safety? We could get a great engagement there.'

He stood biting his nails, agitated.

'There is this last affair to be carried through,' he reminded her. 'And the money—think of it! How can one live without money!'

'Our salaries,' she murmured.

'Pooh! What man with my tastes could live on any salary?'

'Is it worth while to trifle with life and death?' she asked him bluntly. 'It is a warning, this, Henri.'

The call-boy's voice was suddenly heard.

'Monsieur Anders! Monsieur Anders!'

The Frenchman turned mechanically towards the door.

'You have destroyed my nerve,' he muttered. 'You have perhaps ruined my performance. Afterwards we will see.' ...

It was 'French Night' at Luigi's Restaurant, a gala night even in those strenuous war days. Every table in the place was taken, and others had been wheeled in. The waiters made their way about with difficulty. Bohemia and the sycophantic scions of fashion sat arm in arm. The grimmer duties of patriotism were for a moment forgotten. Its other claims met with ample recognition. Félanie sang the 'Marseillaise' twice amidst a scene of wild applause. A great French actress from the legitimate stage had recited a patriotic ode. The flags on the tables had been sold for absurd sums by a sympathetic duke who should clearly have been an auctioneer. A hundred messages of sympathy, of love, of faith, were sent across the wineglasses to the country whom it was designed to honour. Back in their corner, Lavendale and Suzanne looked on curiously. Once Lavendale drank a little toast with his companion.

'This,' he murmured,' is to our fuller alliance.'

She drank with him, although she seemed a little puzzled.

'Listen, dear,' he went on, 'there is just one little thing I'd like to say to you to-night. You and I have helped one another at times, but there has always been a certain reserve. I told you months ago that I was for America above all things, and America only. To-day I feel differently. I have been a witness—you and I together—of foul and brutal murder. I have seen women drowned, have heard their shrieks. America may keep the peace with Germany. It may be in the interests of the highest diplomacy that she should. As for me, I am at war with Germany. I am your ally.'

Her fingers rested upon his.

'Then there is some good,' she whispered, 'which has come out of that great and abominable evil.'

'A very small good,' he said, 'but it may count. Tell me, do you know who that fair, almost sandy young man is, sitting at the table with Félanie and her friends?'

'Of course,' she answered. 'That is Lenwade, the great flying man.'

She dropped her voice suddenly. The young man had risen from his chair, and, in the act of passing down the room to speak to some acquaintances, paused before their table. He bowed to Suzanne and held out his hand to Lavendale. They were old acquaintances and spoke for some time on indifferent subjects.

'What have you been doing with yourself lately?' Lavendale inquired.

'Not much flying,' the other confessed. 'I have been down giving lessons and breaking in a lot of the youngsters, but I can't stick it myself as I used to. Plays the devil with your nerves.'

'Rubbish!' Lavendale laughed. 'You haven't a nerve in your body.'

'Haven't I?' the other replied. 'I remember the time when I could say that. I'd give anything to be at the front now if I felt equal to it, or if my doctor would let me.'

Lavendale smiled, and glanced around to be sure that his neighbours were not listening.

'What were you doing at Ypres the week before last, then?' he asked, dropping his voice a little.

Lenwade for a moment was silent, then he shrugged his shoulders.

'You must have mistaken me for some one else,' he declared. 'Good-night!'

He took his leave a little abruptly. Lavendale watched him disappear. Then he glanced towards his companion. His face had become graver.

'Let me put a case to you, my fellow conspirator,' he begged.

'I will put one to you instead,' she replied. 'I know for a fact that Philip Lenwade has been in France for two months, flying every day, engaged upon some special task. He denies it to us—quite properly, perhaps—but should he come to places like this, should he drink champagne so that he is compelled to hold the table while he stands? It is true that all the world knows of his infatuation for Félanie. She is safe, perhaps—a Frenchwoman and a patriot—yet there is something about it which I do not like. She and Lenwade have been whispering together half the evening, and more than once I have seen Lenwade shake his head and push her away.'

'Supposing Félanie,' he whispered, 'were not a Frenchwoman at all?'

Suzanne said nothing. She waited, watching her companion with wide-open eyes. Lavendale looked down upon the tablecloth.

'From you,' he continued simply, 'I have no secrets. Nine years ago I knew Félanie in Paris. She went then by the name of Adèle Goetz. She was a German.'

'Go on.'

'I watched her from the box to-night. At first I was oppressed, as I have been before, by some vague sense of familiarity in her gestures. Suddenly—I think it was the way she shrugged her shoulders, one higher than the other—anyhow, something brought it all back to me. That was why I left you, Suzanne. I went to her room. Her flaxen hair has become blue-black, she has altered in many ways but I discovered that I was right.'

'She is a German, posing as a Frenchwoman, in London to-day?' Suzanne exclaimed. 'Why does she run this risk?'

'That is what I have asked myself,' he whispered, 'that and another question—what is her interest in Lenwade? Hush! We are talking too earnestly. That fellow Anders—they say he is really her husband—watches us. Here comes Luigi. Talk to him for a moment.'

The manager paused at their table and received their compliments on the success of the evening. When he passed on, Félanie had risen as though to go, and Lenwade was arranging her cloak around her shoulders. Anders was still talking to some other members of the company, and friends seated at the great round table in front of the orchestra. Félanie and Lenwade were half-way down the room before the others began to follow. Lavendale rose quickly to his feet.

'Listen,' he said, 'I am going upstairs and shall come down again just far enough, in case I can hear anything. You go through alone and wait for me on the divan. Tell me if those two go away together, and if so, what is their destination.'

They separated at once. A few minutes later Lavendale descended from the balcony and stood just out of sight upon the stairs which led into the entrance hall. The little place was full of the hubbub of cheerful laughter. On one side, however, Félanie and Lenwade were talking earnestly. Félanie had turned suddenly round to Anders, who had just arrived.

'Mr. Lenwade is going to drive me home,' she announced. 'Au revoir, all you good people!'

There was much handshaking.

'Vive la France, madame,' a young Englishman exclaimed fervently, as he bent over Félanie's fingers, 'and may you, too, live for ever!'

'If one would paint France, madame,' a painter murmured, 'I would choose you for the emblematic figure.'

There were more compliments, another little burst of patriotic fervour. Some one even struck up a few bars of the 'Marseillaise' as Félanie and her escort disappeared. Lavendale descended the last few stairs and elbowed his way good-humouredly through the group. He took Suzanne by the arm.

'Well?' he whispered, as he led her towards the doorway.

'I am not sure,' she answered under her breath, 'but I think they went to his rooms—number 25 Half Moon Street.'

Lavendale's car was a few minutes delayed. He gave the man the address almost in a whisper. Behind, pushing his way out on to the pavement, was Anders. He watched Lavendale drive off with a slightly disturbed air.

'What are you going to do?' Suzanne asked.

'Make a fool of myself, very likely,' Lavendale replied. 'I am just working out a theory, that's all. She is going back to his rooms. Anders remains behind, content, and all the world knows that Anders, whether he is her husband or not, is in love with her and furiously jealous. You see, there must be a reason for her little expedition. She is hoping to fetch something.'

'Where are we going?'

'To his rooms,' Lavendale explained. 'Oh! don't look startled, dear. I shall have a very good explanation to offer to Lenwade, even if I break in upon the most ordinary amour.'

They were in Half Moon Street within a few minutes. Just as Lavendale's car slackened speed, Félanie issued from the door of number 25, and, looking neither to the right nor to the left, sprang into a waiting taxicab and drove off. Lavendale leaped out on to the pavement.

'Follow her, Suzanne,' he directed. 'I hope to God she's going straight home! If not, you must find out where she does go. I'll come in a taxi. I must see Lenwade first.'

He whispered a direction to the chauffeur, passed through the door of number 25, rang for an automatic lift and ascended to the second storey. Leaning over the banisters, as the lift stopped, was Lenwade. He gazed at his visitor in amazement.

'What the mischief are you doing here, old fellow?' he asked thickly.

'Whom are you looking for?' Lavendale retorted.

'Madame Félanie,' the other confessed. 'She has gone down to fetch her vanity case from the cab. Can't think why she doesn't come back.'

Lavendale pushed him suddenly back into his room and closed the door.

'You idiot!' he thundered. 'She isn't coming back! Now pull yourself together, do you hear? Listen to me. You're half drunk, but I am going to tell you something that ought to sober you. That woman Félanie is a born German, and a spy. What have you given her?'

Even through the bluster of his stormy denial, Lenwade was obviously shaken.

'What bally rot!' he exclaimed. 'She's a Frenchwoman to her finger-tips. They all love her. Didn't you hear her sing—Marseillaise? Frenchwoman to her finger——'

'Shut up!' Lavendale interrupted fiercely. 'I tell you I knew her nine years ago under another name. She is a German, and it's my belief she's a spy, she and Anders. What have they worked on you? Out with it, man!'

Lenwade swayed on his feet. He looked back across his shoulder to a roll-top writing desk which stood open. Then he snatched up a tumbler from the table by his side, filled it with soda-water and drank it off.

'Lavendale, you're not in earnest!'

'In God's own earnest, man! Quick, if you want to repair the mischief you've done, tell me what you gave her?'

'I've lent her my plans,' Lenwade faltered. 'I've been two months making them, up above the clouds. I'm the only real draughtsman amongst those who can keep high enough—plans of the German fortifications and the railways behind, from the coast beyond where our lines touch the French. I say, Lavendale——!'

There was no Lavendale. He sprang down the stairs three at a time, out into the street and at a double into Piccadilly, where he sprang into a passing taxicab.

'Milan! Look sharp!' he ordered.

The man drove swiftly through the half-empty streets. With a little gasp of relief Lavendale recognized his own car waiting in the courtyard. Without a pause, however, he pushed open the swing doors of the Court and leaned over the counter towards the night porter.

'What is Madame Félanie's number?' he asked.

'Sixty-four, sir,' the man replied, glancing dubiously at Lavendale. 'Monsieur Anders is up there now, however.'

Lavendale stepped into the lift, ascended to the third floor, hurried down the dimly-lit corridor and paused outside the door of number sixty-four. He listened for a moment. Inside he could hear voices. Then he pressed the bell. There was a moment's hesitation, then Anders' voice speaking in French.

'Lenwade, perhaps.'

He heard Félanie's scornful little laugh, the flutter of her garments as she crossed the room. The door was suddenly opened and she stood there, looking out at him. She gazed at this unexpected visitor and the colour slowly faded from her cheeks and the light from her eyes. Lavendale made his way firmly across the threshold and closed the door. Félanie caught at her throat.

'What do you want here, sir?' Anders demanded.

Lavendale pushed them both back into the sitting-room. There was an ugly look in the man's face, but Félanie's courage seemed to have deserted her. She clutched at the air for a moment and sank into an easy-chair, hiding her face amongst the cushions. Lavendale's hand fell firmly upon the loose sheets of paper strewn over the table.

'These are what I have come for,' he announced, collecting them and thrusting them into his pocket. 'I presume you have had no time to make a copy?'

He glanced searchingly around the apartment. It was obvious that nothing of the sort had been attempted. Anders stole slowly back towards the writing-table, his hand was upon the knob of one of the drawers, but Lavendale suddenly gripped him by the coat collar and swung him almost off his feet.

'Listen,' he said coldly, 'I know nothing of you, Anders, except that it is my belief that you are one of the vermin of the war, a spy selling his own country. The woman there was once my friend. For that reason, if you leave England on Saturday for America, this matter is finished. If either of you remain in London, or make any attempt to cross to Holland, France or any other country, between now and then, something very ugly will happen. You understand?'

Anders' courage had failed him pitifully. Félanie, on the contrary, had recovered herself.

'I have been a fool, perhaps,' she confessed. 'You were just one of the few chances against me. Very well, we go to America on Saturday.'

'But our contract?' Anders faltered. 'The revue? Elaine's success? They have doubled our salaries. London is at her feet.'

'After Saturday,' Lavendale reminded him calmly, 'the best that can happen to you, Anders, is a bandaged forehead and twelve bullets, in the courtyard of the Tower. I will not offend your taste by suggesting— —'

Félanie stamped her foot and turned her shoulder contemptuously upon Anders.

'It is finished, Monsieur Lavendale,' she pronounced. 'If there were any bribe in the world I could offer you——'

It was her one rather faint-hearted effort and he laughed at the seduction in her eyes.

'You will be watched from this moment until the steamer leaves Liverpool,' he concluded, leaving the room and closing the door behind him....

In the hall he met Lenwade, waiting for the lift, incoherent still but sober. Lavendale drew him out into the courtyard, where Suzanne was still seated in the car.

'Lenwade,' he announced, 'I have your plans. They are safe with me. I shall keep them until to-morrow morning. You can come to me at 17 Sackville Street at ten o'clock. Until then they will be safe.'

'Thank God!' the other murmured. 'How did you manage it?'

Lavendale shook him off a little contemptuously and took his place by Suzanne's side.

'They leave on Saturday for Liverpool,' he told her. 'I hand the care of them, from now until then, over to your branch.'

She pressed his hand and drew a little closer to him.

'My dear ally!' she murmured.

CHAPTER X.
THE SENTENCE OF THE COURT

Lavendale was closeted with a Personage, and the interview to which he found himself committed came as something of a shock to him. The Personage was not in the habit of wasting his words, and he spoke succinctly and to the point.

'To sum up, Mr. Lavendale,' he concluded, 'we have received direct and categorical complaints concerning you, forwarded to us through the German Ambassador in Washington. It is stated that whilst enjoying the shelter and privileges of your association with the Embassy here, you have rendered direct aid to a Branch of the French Secret Service in this country, and that you were yourself responsible for the interception of an important communication from Berlin.'

'That's Leonard Johnson,' Lavendale muttered.

'The case of Leonard Johnson has, I believe, been cited,' the Personage admitted, 'but your association with a certain member of the French Secret Service has led you, I am informed, into further enterprises not entirely in accordance with your position as an American official.'

'Am I to understand that you wish me to resign, sir?' Lavendale asked.

'Nothing,' the Personage replied cheerfully, 'is further from my intentions. I wish you to reform. Remember you are an American, that's all. Now go and pay us a visit on the other side. I am coming in to do a little hand-shaking myself presently.'

Lavendale put behind him what he felt might be one of the crises of his life, and made his way to the ambassadorial reception rooms. He paid his respects to his Chief's wife and family and talked for a while to one of the junior secretaries. A clean-shaven man, tall and slim, with gold spectacles and smooth hair, came up to them presently with a smile.

'I hope you haven't quite forgotten me, Mr. Lavendale,' he said. 'I'm Anthony Silburn. Four years before your time, but we've met once or twice in New York.'

'Of course,' Lavendale assented. 'As a matter of fact, we are connections, aren't we? You married my cousin, Lydia Green.'

They sat in a corner and talked for some time of common acquaintances. Mr. Anthony Silburn, besides having the advantage of a frank and engaging manner and a distinct sense of humour, was, as Lavendale very well knew, one of the wealthiest and most enlightened of American millionaires.

'I tell you what it is, young fellow,' Mr. Silburn declared, as they parted, 'you'll have to come down and spend a week-end with us, any time you like. I've got a real old country house in Norfolk—leased it before the war broke out—Hookam Court, near Wells. Bring your guns down. Well, I'm off now to catch the five o'clock train home.'

He departed, with a little farewell nod. Lavendale looked after him thoughtfully.

'One of the most successful men in America,' somebody by his side remarked. 'I wonder what he thinks about the war. He was educated in Germany—I am not sure that he wasn't born there.'

Lavendale made his adieux a little later and walked thoughtfully towards the Milan Court. He sent his name up, but there was no reply from Suzanne's rooms.

'Miss de Freyne went out on Monday night,' the hall-porter told him. 'She was motoring, I think, but she had very little luggage. She hasn't been back since. We've had a great many telephone messages for her.'

The circumstance was not in itself unusual, but Lavendale was conscious of a queer little feeling of uneasiness. Suzanne never left town without letting him know and she had been engaged to dine with him that night.

'I think I'll go up and speak to her maid,' he said.

The man pointed towards the lift.

'There she is, sir, just come in.'

Lavendale crossed the hall and touched the woman on the shoulder. She was a dark-visaged, melancholy-looking person of middle age, with an extraordinary gift for taciturnity.

'Do you know where your mistress is, Anne?' he asked.

The woman appeared to recognize him with some relief. She evaded a direct reply, however.

'Would you be so kind as to come upstairs, sir?' she invited.

Lavendale followed her to Suzanne's suite. She stood on one side for him to enter and closed the door carefully.

'Monsieur,' she began, 'my mistress once told me that if there was trouble I was to come to you.'

'Quite right,' Lavendale assented quickly. 'What is it?'

'Mademoiselle left me at six o'clock on Monday night,' the maid proceeded. 'I know nothing as to her destination except that her journey was decided upon quite suddenly and that she had a motor ride of over a hundred miles. She expected to be back the next day. If not, she promised to send me some instructions. Since then I have heard nothing of her.'

Lavendale reflected for a moment.

'How much are you in your mistress' confidence?' he inquired.

'She has trusted me often with her life,' was the quiet reply.

'You understand her real position?'

'But naturally.'

'Then do you know,' Lavendale went on, 'if there is any headquarters of the French Secret Service in this country—any one from whom we could get any idea as to her mission?'

The woman shook her head.

'There are others working often with Mademoiselle,' she said. 'I know no names—only this. In case of the very deepest anxiety, but only in extremes, I have a telephone number here which I could ring up.'

She opened her purse and drew out a slip of paper.

'It is, I believe, a private number,' she continued, 'and not in the book. I made up my mind that if Mademoiselle had not returned this afternoon, I would ring up.'

'Let us do so at once,' Lavendale suggested.

'If monsieur would be so kind,' she begged, pointing to the instrument. 'My English is not good, and I do not know with whom I should speak.'

'Whom am I to ask for?' Lavendale inquired.

'No names are to be mentioned,' the woman replied, 'and the number can only be rung up between five and seven. It is six o'clock now,' she added.

Lavendale took off the receiver and asked for the number. There was a moment's pause. Then a remarkably clear voice answered him.

'Well?'

'It is a friend of Mademoiselle de Freyne who speaks,' Lavendale said.

'That is well,' the voice replied. 'Continue.'

'Miss de Freyne left her rooms at the Milan Court last Monday night, on secret business. She promised to communicate with her maid the next day. She has not done so. She left in a motor-car and with very little luggage. She made the remark that she had a ride of over a hundred miles.'

'That is all you know, Mr. Lavendale?'

Lavendale started a little at the sound of his own name.

'It is all,' he assented.

'Kindly go and repeat what you have told me to Major Elwell, room 17, number 33, Whitehall.'

Lavendale replaced the receiver and turned to Anne.

'I am instructed,' he said, 'to apply to a man whom I know to be in the English Secret Service.'

'It would be well,' the maid advised, 'if monsieur applied there at once.'

Lavendale walked briskly out of the Milan by the back exit, through the Gardens, along the Embankment and into Whitehall. He found number 33 a long, narrow, private house taken over by the Government. Number 17 consisted of a small office in which two men were busy writing, and an inner room. Lavendale made his inquiry and was told that Major Elwell would be back in an hour. He scribbled a note, making an appointment, and walked back to his own rooms.

He let himself in, paused to speak for a moment with his servant, who was laying out his clothes, and turned towards the sitting-room. As he opened the door the telephone bell began to ring insistently. He crossed the room, took up the receiver, and tapped the instrument.

'What is it?' he asked. 'Hullo? Hullo?'

Somewhere in the distance he heard a voice say faintly—'Trunk call'—and for a moment he was patient. Then he gave a little start. A familiar voice, yet unfamiliar, shaking with something like fear, tremulous, hysterical, terrified, murmured his name. His heart leapt with quick sympathy, his fingers shook.

'Ambrose! Ambrose! Is that you? Speak quickly!'

'I am here, Suzanne,' he cried. 'Where are you?'

Suddenly he seemed to hear turmoil and confusion, a man's voice, a woman's shriek.

'At Hook——'

Then there was silence. The connection had been broken. Lavendale rang up furiously. At last he got the exchange. The young man who answered his inquiry could tell him nothing. He rang through to the inquiry office with little better result. They would make inquiries and let him know from whence the call came. They believed that it was from a call office. He could gain no further information. He set down the instrument at last in despair and walked up and down the room. She was in trouble, danger. 'Hook—?' 'Hook—?' What was there familiar to him in the commencement of that word? He repeated it feverishly. Then he remembered—Hookam Court—Anthony Silburn, whom he had met that afternoon at the Embassy. It was hard to discover any connection, however. He drove back to the Milan Court and found Anne.

'Is there any news, monsieur?' she asked anxiously.

'None at present,' Lavendale replied. 'I cannot see Major Elwell for another half-hour. Tell me, have you ever heard your mistress mention any place of which the first syllable is "Hook"?'

'"Ook,"' Anne repeated dubiously. 'No, monsieur!'

'Hookam Court,' Lavendale went on, 'Anthony Silburn—Norfolk—none of that is familiar?'

'But no, monsieur!'

He kept the secret of the telephone message to himself and made his way round once more to Whitehall. Major Elwell was seated in his office and received him at once. There was nothing unusual about the place except a large array of telephones. Lavendale told his story quickly. The Major listened without comment.

'Well?' Lavendale asked eagerly, when he had finished.

Major Elwell was occupied in drawing small diagrams with his pencil on the edge of the blotting-paper.

'We must see what can be done,' he remarked at last. 'Hook'— that is absolutely all you heard?'

'Absolutely,' Lavendale assured him.

'And you have a friend who lives at Hookam Court in Norfolk— Mr. Anthony Silburn?' he said meditatively. 'A very remarkable man, Silburn—likely to be President some day, they tell me.'

'Who cares about that!' Lavendale exclaimed, a little curtly. 'What can we do, Major Elwell? I dare say you know as much as I do, and more. Miss de Freyne has been very successful during the last few months, and there is no doubt they'd give anything they could to get hold of her on the other side. But in England—surely there can't be any organization over here strong enough for actual mischief!'

'Scarcely,' Major Elwell agreed. 'Scarcely. 'H—double O—K,' he went on meditatively. 'You see, there are about fifty places in the United Kingdom beginning like that.'

Lavendale felt his courage slipping away. There was something curiously unimpressive in the carefully-dressed, imperturbable Englishman, who was occupied now in polishing his eyeglass.

'Isn't there anything we can be doing instead of sitting here talking?' he asked impatiently.

'Always a mistake,' Major Elwell declared, 'to do things in a hurry. Have a cigarette,' he went on, offering his case. 'I think I'll stroll out and talk with a friend over this little matter.'

'Isn't there a thing I can do?' Lavendale persisted.

'Well,' Major Elwell said thoughtfully, 'you spoke of an invitation to visit your friend Mr. Anthony Silburn at Hookam Court. Why not motor down there to-morrow? It's one of the places in the country that your call might have come from, at any rate.'

A derisive reply quivered upon Lavendale's lips. Then, for some reason or other, he changed his mind and remained silent. Major Elwell, without any appearance of hurrying him, was holding the door open.

'All right,' Lavendale agreed, 'I'll motor down there to-morrow.'

*****

Lavendale was conscious of a queer sensation of unreality as late on the following afternoon he followed the butler across the white-flagged entrance hall of Hookam Court. He felt as though he were an unwilling actor in a play of which the setting was all too perfect. The little party of guests, still in shooting clothes and lounging before the great wood fire, brought into their surroundings a vivid note of flamboyant artificiality. The high walls, with their ecclesiastically-curved frescoes, the row of family portraits, the armour standing in the recesses, even the little local touch afforded by the game-keeper in brown whipcord and gaiters, standing waiting in a distant corner, seemed to him like part of some cinema production in which the men and women were supers and the setting tinsel.

His host's greeting was all that it should have been. He advanced across the hall with outstretched hand, quietly but sincerely cordial.

'Good man, Lavendale!' he exclaimed. 'I was delighted to get your telegram.'

'Very nice of you,' Lavendale murmured. 'I hadn't any idea of being at a loose end so soon when you were kind enough to ask me.'

'It couldn't have happened more fortunately,' Mr. Anthony Silburn assured him. 'I've another man coming down to-night, but I've room for two more guns. Now let me introduce you to those of your fellow-guests whom you don't know. Mr. Lavendale—Lady Marsham, Mr. Kindersley, Mr. Barracombe, Sir Julius Marsham, Mr. Henry D. Steinletter.'

Lavendale bowed, individually to the women and collectively to the men. Lady Marsham, a stout, dark-haired lady with a heavy jaw, made room for him by her side.

'It is quite a treat, Mr. Lavendale,' she declared, 'to see a young man. One feels that he must be either an American or a hopeless invalid. You are an American, aren't you?'

Lavendale admitted the fact and rose to welcome his hostess, who was coming down the stairs. She suddenly recognized Lavendale and stopped short. For the first time he was conscious of something which freed him from that sense of being part of a carefully concerted picture. There was something absolutely human, entirely spontaneous in his cousin's expression as she recognized him. Her fingers gripped the oak banisters, her lips were parted, her eyes were filled with something which was scarcely a welcoming light. It all passed in a moment and she came into the picture naturally and easily.

'My dear Ambrose, how delightful to see you again! Does Tony know?'

Lavendale advanced to meet her and took her hands.

'He asked me down for a few days only yesterday, when I met him in town, and I wired to say that I was coming to-day. I am afraid I didn't give him a chance to turn me down, but I meant to say, although he hasn't given me an opportunity yet, that if it's at all inconvenient I could go on to Norwich and look up some friends near there.

For a single moment she hesitated. Her little laugh was not altogether natural. Again Lavendale had a queer fancy that there was a leaven of insincerity in her welcome—that if it had been possible she would even have sent him away.

'Don't be foolish, Ambrose. Of course we are delighted. I see you people have had tea,' she went on. 'I really couldn't resist a bath and tea-gown.'

'And I was much too lazy,' Lady Marsham yawned, lighting a cigarette. 'I shall go up and change early for dinner.'

Mr. Silburn's voice was heard from the other end of the hall. He was dismissing the game-keeper with a few parting instructions.

'I'll have another covering stand at the long wood, Reynolds,' he was saying. 'You can put it on the extreme left, near the old oak. I'll take that myself, and Mr. Lavendale will shoot from number three. You've got your guns, Lavendale?' he added, strolling up to them.

'They are in the car,' Lavendale replied, 'but I warn you that I haven't shot for two years.'

'I don't think my pheasants will bother you any,' Mr. Silburn promised him. 'Barracombe here finds them on the slow side. We had a very good day to-day—over a thousand head altogether. Sure you won't have some tea or a whisky-and-soda?'

'Nothing, thanks.'

'Then I'll show you your rooms,' his host continued, 'if you'll come this way.'

Lydia Silburn, who had been standing a little irresolutely on the other side of the round tea-table, suddenly turned towards her husband.

'Why didn't you tell me, Tony, that Ambrose was coming?' she inquired.

'I meant to,' her husband admitted. 'As it happens, however, I haven't seen much of you to-day, have I? Come along, young fellow. Did you bring a servant, by-the-by? No? Well, I've quite a smart second boy who can look after you. We dine at eight. And, Lavendale, just one word,' he concluded, as he glanced around the spacious rooms into which he had ushered his guest, 'we have a sort of unwritten rule to which every one subscribes here. It saves so much unpleasant argument on a subject where our opinions are a little divided. We don't mention the war until half-past ten.'

'Very sound,' Lavendale remarked, 'but why half-past ten?'

'After dinner,' Mr. Silburn promised, 'I will explain that to you. We have a little conversazione sometimes—but just wait.' ...

Again, an hour or so later, when Lavendale stood once more in the hall talking to one or two of the men, whilst a footman was passing round cock-tails upon a tray, he felt oppressed by that curious sense of unreality. He took himself severely to task for it. He told himself that it must lie simply in the innate incongruity of this occupation of a ducal home by an American millionaire. In every other respect the men and women were obviously fitting figures. One or two of them were even known to him by reputation. The whole atmosphere of their conversation was natural and spontaneous. And then, as he turned resolutely to continue a discussion about wild pheasants with Barracombe—Barracombe, whom he knew well to be a great scientific traveller, a man of distinction—it was then that the climax came, the dramatic note which alone was needed to convince him of the spuriousness of his surroundings. He had turned his head quite naturally towards the broad, western corridor on hearing the soft rustling of a woman's skirts—and he talked no more of wild pheasants! It was Suzanne, in a black evening gown and carrying a handful of pink roses in her hand, who was coming slowly across the hall.

'Suzanne! Miss de Freyne!' he exclaimed, taking a quick step forward.

He was conscious of many things in those few seconds, conscious of his host's strenuous regard, of Suzanne's unnatural pallor, of the warning in her eyes. His rush of joy at seeing her, however, was all-conquering. He took her hands in his and held them tightly.

'And to think that no one told me you were here!' he exclaimed.

There was a moment's strained silence. Then a cold wave of doubt, a premonition of evil, suddenly chilled him. In the background he had caught a glimpse of a peculiar smile upon his host's lips, and again there was the warning in Suzanne's eyes.

'I have been down in the neighbourhood for several days,' she told him. 'It is rather a coincidence, is it not?'

Anthony Silburn, who had remained all the time within earshot, strolled over towards them.

'So you young people have discovered one another,' he remarked. 'The gong at last!' he added, with a little burst of enthusiasm. 'Lavendale, as it is your first evening, will you take Lydia in? Miss de Freyne, I am going to give myself the happiness to-night.'

He held out his arm and led Suzanne away. Lavendale loitered behind with his cousin.

'Lydia,' he whispered, as they passed into the great dining-room, 'how long has Miss de Freyne been here?'

'In this house since the day before yesterday,' she answered. 'She was staying before at the Hookam Arms, down in the village.'

'Say, is there anything wrong about this place?' he asked. 'I don't know what it is, but I feel as though I'd come into some sort of a theatrical performance. I suppose you are all alive, aren't you? That really is Barracombe, the traveller, and old Steinletter?'

His tone had been one of half banter, but her reply made him suddenly serious.

'I don't know, Ambrose,' she confessed nervously. 'Sometimes I feel like that myself. Don't talk too loudly.'

Lavendale became a watcher through the progress of the wonderfully served meal. The servants, in a way, were all of the usual type, obviously well-trained and attentive. The dining-room at Hookam had been built out by a favourite of one of the Georges almost in the form of a pagoda, and under the high, domed roof, listening to the somewhat stereotyped conversation of those strangely-assorted guests, Lavendale became slowly conscious of a new sensation, the sensation of restriction. It was hard to believe that outside lay the park; that in the morning he would be wandering about, free to come and go as he pleased; that in the garage was his own car, and a couple of miles away across the park, the road to London. He tried to talk lightly to Lydia of their relatives and friends in America, but he found her distraite and depressed. Dinner was no sooner over, however, than he made a bold attempt to dissipate some of his presentiments.

'Can I use the telephone, Silburn?' he asked.

'With pleasure, my dear boy,' was the unhesitating reply. 'You'll find an instrument this way.'

They were all crossing the hall. The men and the women were to smoke and take their coffee together. Silburn led his young guest into a small waiting-room, comfortably furnished. On a table in the middle of the apartment was a telephone instrument and a book of subscribers. Lavendale took up the receiver.

'Can you get through to London?' he asked.

'Sorry, sir, the line is engaged,' the operator regretted.

'Will it be free presently?'

'I'll ring up as soon as we can get through. What number?'

Lavendale gave the number of his own rooms and rejoined the little group in the hall. He found Barracombe on one side of Suzanne and his host on the other, but he drew a chair as near to her as he could.

'Get through all right?' Silburn inquired.

'I didn't get through anywhere,' Lavendale replied. 'The line was engaged.'

'We've a lot of soldiers down here,' Mr. Silburn explained. 'They are always commandeering the line for military purposes.'

'You seem to get plenty of messages,' Lavendale remarked, as a servant for the third or fourth time brought a slip of folded paper to his master.

Silburn smiled.

'I have a private line,' he announced. 'Sorry I can't ask you to use it, but I have promised the military here that no one else save myself shall communicate by means of it. Are you a bridger, Lavendale?'

Lavendale excused himself, but gained nothing, for Suzanne was almost forced into the game by her host. He wandered about the hall, glancing up at the pictures. Then he went back to the telephone room.

'Line's still engaged, sir,' was the laconic reply to his inquiry.

Lavendale strolled back. He wandered uneasily about the hall for a time and then approached the great front door.

'Think I'll have a look at the night,' he remarked, with his hand upon the bolt.

The servant who was standing by, intervened.

'I beg your pardon, sir,' he said, 'we are not allowed to open the front door after dusk. The military have complained so much about the lights.'

'Show me another way out from the back, then?' Lavendale persisted.

'No one is allowed to leave the house at all until morning,' the man told him.

Lavendale turned slowly round towards the bridge-table.

'Silburn,' he asked, 'are we prisoners?'

'My dear fellow,' his host replied, dealing out a hand, 'it is not I who am to blame, but the English military authorities. Look how closely-curtained we are everywhere. You will find double blinds in every room in the house. Yet even that has not been enough to satisfy them. I have had to promise that no members of my household shall even open a door after dark. "Defence of the Realm Act" they call it, I think.'

Lavendale turned a little discontentedly away. It was difficult to protest further, but he was not in the least satisfied that Silburn's explanation was a genuine one. He talked for a few moments to several of the other guests and then drew a low chair up close to Suzanne. It was evident to him, watching her closely, that she was playing under great tension. More than ever he was convinced that something was wrong. With an excuse about fetching some cigarettes of a particular brand, he made up to his room and searched in his dressing-case. Within a few minutes he found himself face to face with a very grim reality. The revolver which he carried always with him had been removed! ...

Lavendale, with small hopes of any success, called once more at the telephone room before he rejoined the little party. The reply was almost brusque.

'Line blocked. No chance of getting through to London to-night.'

'Can I ring up Norwich?' Lavendale asked, with a sudden inspiration.

'Line to Norwich engaged,' was the reply.

'Is there anywhere I can speak to?' Lavendale persisted. 'Is there any number upon the exchange I can be connected with?'

There was no reply. He rang again and tapped the wire. There was still silence. Then he replaced the receiver upon the instrument and stood for a moment in the little room, thinking. There was no doubt but that he had simply followed Suzanne into a trap. He rapidly reviewed in his memory the guests. Lady Marsham, it was well known, had been educated in Berlin and had German relatives. Barracombe wore an order conferred upon him by the Kaiser. Steinletter belonged to the greatest German-American banking firm in the world. Kindersley's daughter had married an Austrian prince. Suzanne had succeeded, then, in this last quest of hers, a success which, although inadvertently, he might be said to share. They had in all probability discovered the headquarters of the great Teutonic espionage system in England. How was it going to profit them? His mind rapidly reviewed the situation. They were prisoners—of that he was certain—yet to what extent? How far was Silburn prepared to go? It was, after all, rather an opera-bouffe sort of trap. If they were caught, there was still the question of silencing them. Then he thought of that abstracted revolver, and a queer little wave of apprehension, not for himself but for Suzanne, suddenly chilled him.

He made his way back into the hall. The rubber was just over and he leaned boldly over the chair in which Suzanne was seated.

'Come and talk to me for a few minutes,' he begged.

She hesitated. Mr. Silburn, who was playing idly with the cards, glanced at the clock and back again.

'At half-past ten,' he announced, 'in ten minutes, that is to say, we all meet in the cloister room. It is a queer custom, perhaps, but my guests have been kind in conforming to it.'

'Prayers?' Lavendale inquired.

'Not a bad name for our few minutes' serious diversion,' Mr. Silburn remarked dryly.

Lavendale led Suzanne towards a couch at the further end of the hall. He laid his hand upon hers and found it as cold as ice.

'Suzanne,' he said quietly, 'are we in a trap?'

'I believe we are,' she answered. 'It is entirely my fault. I have never been so foolish before in my life. I have always had people behind me who have known my whereabouts and who could come to the rescue, if necessary. This time I told no one. I was selfish. I wanted the whole credit. But tell me of yourself — how you came here?'

'It was just the merest chance,' he replied. 'Silburn had asked me to shoot here, and then you half told me where you were, over the telephone. I think that the rest must have been instinct. You haven't told me yet, though, how you found your way here?'

'I was down at the village,' she said. 'I followed Mr. Steinletter here. I had a special permit, a military pass. I was supposed to be related to one of the officers quartered at the inn. I made a few inquiries about this place, which increased my suspicions. Then I met Mrs. Silburn outside the lodge gates. She was with the Colonel in command here and they stopped to speak to the officer I was with. She was delightful and asked me to call. I was only too glad to have a chance of obtaining the entrée to the house. They made me send for my clothes, to spend the night. That was two days ago. Since then I have tried in vain to get away.'

'Let me understand what you mean by trying to get away?' he begged. 'Surely you could ask for a car to take you to the station?'

'I have done so three times,' she replied, 'always with the same result. They assure me that every car in the garage has been requisitioned by the Government. I go to that dummy telephone—the exchange is in the house, you know—and of course nothing happens. If I start out to walk, I am shadowed by one of the men-servants, and, as you know, it is two miles before one reaches the road.'

'Well, there isn't much they can do with us, dear,' Lavendale assured her coolly. 'Tell me now, have you made any actual discovery?'

'There is a private telegraph and telephone exchange here in the place,' she said, 'and Mr. Silburn gets messages every few hours. There are people always coming and going, all people of the same class. There is not the slightest doubt that this is the place for which we have searched. Ambrose, if only we could stretch out the net now, at this moment, we could make a great haul.'

'Instead of which,' he remarked grimly, 'we seem to be in the meshes ourselves!'

'Tell me,' she begged, 'does any one know that you were coming here?'

'I told Elwell—Major Elwell,' Lavendale replied, with a suddenly inspired flash of memory. 'I told him why I was coming here, too.'

She clutched at his arm. Then suddenly she looked down. 'They are watching us,' she whispered. 'Ambrose, that may save us yet if only he comes in time!'

'In time for what?' Lavendale answered cheerfully. 'I can't look upon this as very serious, dear. Why, Lydia Silburn is my own cousin.'

'She is our only hope,' Suzanne declared. 'As for the rest, I have grown to suspect every one of them.'

'What does this half-past ten business mean?' he asked.

She shook her head.

'At half-past ten they all go into what they call the cloister room,' she said. 'As yet I have not been invited there, but I have an idea that to-night we are both to be present. Yes, here comes Mr. Silburn.'

'Now, you young people,' their host observed pleasantly, 'we are going to let you into a few secrets. This way.'

They both rose. The others were crossing the hall towards the eastern corridor. Mr. Silburn drew Suzanne's arm through his. As they walked his face became more serious. Lavendale had a wild idea, for a moment, of snatching Suzanne away, opening the front door by force and clamouring for freedom. Then he remembered the two miles to the lodge gate and shrugged his shoulders.

'It's rather a queer apartment into which I am going to take you,' Mr. Silburn explained, 'a crazy sort of place, really, but to us Americans this sort of room, I must confess, appeals some. Allow me, Miss de Freyne.'

He motioned them both to precede him. They found themselves in what seemed to be, from the bareness of the walls and the shape of the windows, a small chapel, built on different levels. The larger part of the room, which was below, was wrapped in complete gloom. The smaller part was unfurnished save for a long table, around which was ranged a number of chairs. One by one, the guests seated themselves. Lavendale and Suzanne followed their example as indifferently as possible. Mr. Silburn sat at the head of the table, with Lady Marsham on his right and Mr. Steinletter opposite. There was a certain significance to Lavendale in the fact that his cousin was not present. A somewhat gloomy light was thrown upon the faces of the little company from a heavily-shaded oil lamp suspended by a brass chain from the roof, and, looking around at their mingled expressions, Lavendale for the first time felt a sense of real danger, a thrill of something like fear, not for his own sake but for Suzanne's. He groped for her hand beneath the table and held the icy-cold fingers tightly.

'Courage, dear,' he murmured under his breath.

She smiled at him plaintively, and with the fear still lurking in her dark eyes. Then Mr. Silburn leaned forward in his place and tapped upon the table with his forefinger. His voice in the hollow spaces sounded strangely.

'My friends,' he began, 'few words are best. We live, as you all know, from day to day in danger. No such association as ours could continue to exist without hourly peril. So far we have triumphed over the secret service of every country. So far we have carried on our great work without hindrance or suspicion. Those days I am forced to tell you, are passing. The hour of our supreme peril is close at hand.

There are two people here present who have guessed our secret. One of them, this young lady upon my left, Miss de Freyne, is here for no other purpose than to spy upon us.'

Suzanne seemed to have regained her courage. In the moment of trial she was stronger than in the indeterminate hours of suspense. She turned her head towards Silburn.

'What are you all but spies,' she demanded, 'spies of the lowest and most dastardly class? You are here under the shelter of a friendly country to do her all the harm you can, to stab in the dark, to take advantage of your nationality—your American nationality—to pose as an Anglo-Saxon. You abuse the country which shelters you. You call me a spy! Compared with you, all of you, I am the most innocent person who ever breathed.'

A strange impassivity seemed to be reflected from all the faces of the little gathering. Only in Mr. Kindersley's face there trembled for a moment some shadow of sympathy.

'You have heard the young lady,' Mr. Silburn continued calmly. 'We come now to her companion. Mr. Lavendale, although an American by birth, has embraced the cause of this country; doubtless,' he added, with a little satirical bow, 'for reasons upon which I will not enlarge. He has become the ally of mademoiselle. We secured his presence here, I admit, by a ruse. My friends, these two people's knowledge of our secret is fatal to our safety.'

There was a moment's silence. Then Lady Marsham leaned back in her chair.

'I propose,' she said firmly, 'that the same steps be taken with these two people as heretofore.'

There was a little murmur of approval. Only Mr. Kindersley sighed.

'One must remember,' he observed reflectively, 'that it is not only for our own safety—it is for the preservation of a great cause.'

Lavendale took a cigarette from a box in the centre of the table, and lit it.

'I don't know what this penalty is that you propose to inflict upon us,' he remarked, 'but I should just like to remind you that you are living in a very highly civilized country, where people do not disappear.'

'At Hookam,' Mr. Silburn said calmly, 'people have disappeared for the last nine hundred years. Below there, the secret cloisters reach almost to the sea. The cleverest and most astute criminologists who ever breathed might track you to these doors, Lavendale, and search until their hair was grey before they discovered a single trace of you. My servants are mine, body and soul. For my wife's sake, Lavendale——'

'Look here,' Lavendale interrupted, 'I am not sure whether you are in earnest or not, but whatever you might be thinking about for me, you couldn't be such brutes——'

He stopped short. There was a sudden light in his face. From outside the door they could clearly hear the sound of an angry voice. A little ripple of terrified excitement flashed around the table. Mr. Silburn's teeth came together with a little click. There was a curious tremor of emotion in his tone.

'Lock the door,' he ordered Barracombe.

It was too late. In a long travelling ulster, with his cap still in his hand, Major Elwell stood already upon the threshold. Behind him, still protesting, was Lydia Silburn.

'Elwell!' Lavendale shouted. 'Thank God!'

Major Elwell gazed around at them all through his eye-glass and looked back at the woman by his side. He seemed bewildered.

'What in the name of all that's holy is this?' he demanded.

There was a moment's silence. Lavendale drew a long breath. His arm was stretched out accusingly towards his host. Suddenly the words failed upon his lips. He looked around him, speechless, amazed. It was as though the whole world had gone mad. Mr. Barracombe, from the opposite side of the table, had removed his spectacles from his nose and was wiping the tears from his eyes. Lady Marsham was leaning on one side, doubled up. There was only one common sound everywhere—laughter, irresistible, compelling, unmistakable. Mr. Silburn, taking off his pince-nez and struggling for composure, rose to his feet.

'The sentence of the court upon you two,' he declared unsteadily, 'would have been delivered with more solemnity but for the premature arrival of our friend Jack Elwell. I hereby pronounce it, however, finally and irrevocably. It is this, Ambrose Lavendale—that you offer your arm to Miss de Freyne, that you lead the way in to supper, and that you produce your marriage certificate within three weeks.'

Almost as he spoke, lights flashed out from the great room below. A long table was laid for supper. There were servants who seemed to appear like magic, with bottles and dishes. Lavendale turned towards Elwell, looked back at his host and finally down at Suzanne.

'Suzanne,' he exclaimed, 'I believe we're spoofed!'

She shook her head. There were tears of relief in her eyes, but a delicious curve of laughter upon her lips.

'I do not know the word,' she admitted, 'but I believe it is true.'

'Lead the way, young fellow,' Mr. Silburn insisted. 'Forgive us, you two, but when we heard of Miss de Freyne down at the village, making inquiries about us—well, you remember I had to leave Harvard for a practical joke!'

'All the same,' Lydia Silburn declared from the background, 'the sentence of the court is final.'

They took their places, and the supper party very soon became a much gayer meal than the dinner which had preceded it. Towards its close, Lavendale whispered to Suzanne.

'Dear,' he said, 'I'm afraid we'll have to own up that we haven't been quite as astute as usual. Perhaps we are getting a little stale. Supposing we take—a holiday?'

She flashed a wonderful smile up at him.

'It was the sentence of the court,' she murmured.

THE END